# Barbarians Vs Rome

## Our Lost Legion

## and the Barbarian King

## who Conquered Rome

Claude Stahl

This is a historical novel with its roots in the beginning of the 5th century.

# CHAPTERS

# Chapter I

The young man was excited, his blond hair had been shorn only hours ago and the air felt cool against his scalp. He was waiting in the torch-lit marble hall of the grand villa, where it was now a pleasantly cool evening. The centuries-old mosaics on the walls portrayed gorgeous, colourful Roman gods and mystical animals, and amazed him with their detail and intensity. Some of them he couldn't even identify. A few feet from him, two attentive guards stood in front of the entrance to the inner chamber.

Apart from the guards, he was alone and would soon meet Flavius Vitus, an important and wealthy man who had recently become senator, a man who he had to listen to and obey for the next few weeks. The eerie silence of the sparsely-lit hall gave him an unsettling feeling.

When he had been waiting for hours, a guard finally approached and gestured him towards the entrance of an adjacent hall. The double oak doors opened slowly, and an older bald man stood before him wearing a white toga and a friendly smile.

"Senator Flavius Vitus," the guard announced loudly, pointing to a leather stool where the young man could sit.

Flavius Vitus was a proud, tall man with Nordic rather than Latin facial features. His aura seemed that of a dignified general, with slow steps and deliberate movements. He moved toward the young man, who rose from his chair and knelt before him, leaning one arm on his knee.

"Sit down and listen to me carefully," said Vitus in a commanding tone, nodding at the stool. It was clear that this was not a man accustomed to being told no. "Young man, you are Prince Theodoric, son of King Theodemir of the Ostrogoths. I welcome you to my care; your journey from Constantinople must have been arduous. Have you managed to regain your strength?"

Theodoric, who had just reached man's age, had to smile back. This man, of whom he had already heard so much, radiated dignity but, somehow, he felt he could trust him.

Vitus handed him a jug of water. "Prince Theodoric, as you know, you will be staying with me for some time. You will come to know Rome and learn under my guidance. Later tonight, General Augustus Marcian will arrive and we will share the responsibility of educating you as we have been instructed by the Emperor. We will begin your lessons tonight. However, as you might have heard, my ways of teaching can be considered rather informal and you will learn lessons directly from our experience as soldiers and teachers."

"Thank you Sire," young Theodoric stuttered nervously. "I am humbled and honoured to learn from you."

The senator nodded and surveyed the boy from head to toe.

"What do you know about me?"

"That you are the greatest teacher in the Roman Empire. They say you have influence over the affairs in Africa and that even the Vandal king listens to you."

"Very well. You seem to have already been taught by my colleagues. Over the next couple of weeks, I will be your magister. Mainly, we will discuss Roman law, but you will also be educated in Graeco-Roman values and the glorious history of the Empire. Afterwards, you will return to Constantinople, where your education will continue under the guidance of the Church. If you have questions, ask them now."

The young man looked closely at the senator, noticing a deep scar on his cheek, a sign that Vitus must have been a soldier before rising to the position of senator. "Sire, if I may ask, there are rumours that the city is in danger – are we safe here?"

Vitus raised his head in surprise. "Rome in danger? No, I don't think so." The old man started to open an amphora of wine. "Are you referring to the rumours that the Vandals could attack us under the leadership of King Gaiseric? Don't be afraid, nothing will happen to us."

"Is it true that the Vandals have destroyed, burned, and tortured their way from Germania to Africa?" he asked in a low, scared voice.

Vitus had to smirk in disbelief. "It couldn't be further from the truth. How would you feel if we Romans said this about your people, the cruel and uncouth Ostrogoths?

Theoderic's face darkened. "With respect, Sire, I'd say this would be unforgiving slander. Why should anyone lie about my people?"

Vitus nodded and then grinned in agreement. "Well, some people must lie to protect their own reputation, and others are just unable or unwilling to tell the truth."

"So what are these Vandals like?"

"You could say they are a proud and straight-forward people, ruthless if they must be, and maybe even as powerful as Rome. A bright minded king who will do everything in his power to weaken Rome and settle his people in Roman territory."

"And who is this king?" interrupted the young man, raising his voice. He still felt fearful despite the senator's reassurance.

"A good question. I can tell you a lot about him, and maybe we should start with this king as I believe you could learn something from him as well. How old are you, young man?"

"I have just reached my sixteenth year, Sire.'

"A good age to be. And you are an Ostrogoth, but one day I hope that you will be more Roman than anything else. I will tell you something young man. I was once in a similar position to you, a student and maybe a bit of a barbarian as well, because my mother came from the north, so I knew a little Gothic. And later, I was tribune but after that my destiny changed and I became a teacher, much against my will, because it was I who taught Latin to the King of Kings. You understand?"

"You mean King Gaiseric in Carthage?"

"I'm impressed that you grasped this so quickly. What else do you know about Africa?"

"They call it the granary of Rome – an important province, Sire."

"Not just an important province, it was once our most important province. But sadly, not anymore. Do you know why?"

Theodoric shook his head, embarrassed at his lack of knowledge.

"I'll tell you," Vitus got up and slowly began to pace across the hall. "Once again we're having trouble there because of this Gaiseric and his Vandals. A barbarian people, more powerful than your father's people, they have occupied the African province and regularly make pirate raids on our coasts. Their king seems more cunning and stronger than anyone I have ever encountered. The largest city in the west, the holy city of Carthage, has fallen under their occupation, thereby threatening Rome. One day their fleet could appear before Portus Magnus."

For a second, Vitus stared at the boy appraisingly, "Don't worry, we're all safe here."

"Sire, please forgive my curiosity," Theodoric said eagerly. "But where do these Vandals come from? And is this Gaiseric truly such a great and wise king as my father?"

Vitus had to laugh inside at the naivety of the young man. He stepped over to a console table and filled a goblet with wine from the amphora. "When I think of their king, I shudder out of respect and reverence for him. I have known the king since he was almost as old as you are now. At that time, I served in Germania in the north of the Empire. I was an officer on the Rhine, a mighty river that separated us from the barbarians. So yes, I know this Gaiseric quite well. The truth is that he could be a very dangerous enemy to Rome, but he is also a wise king."

Theodoric shook his head in disbelief. "And this king came down from Germania and now rules all of Africa?"

Again, Vitus scrutinized the young man. "You're old enough to learn things of great importance, so you're already old enough for a cup of wine, aren't you?"

Vitus filled another goblet of wine and presented it to Theodoric. "Drink now. As an old teacher and commander, I also like to speak freely without being deceived or judged, as is common here in this city. This king, Gaiseric, is the lord of two peoples, the Vandals and the Alans. He is a man who has walked the farthest path imaginable and taught us lessons to the point that us Romans actually fear him. A limping bastard who managed to build a mighty Empire in Africa out of nothing.

"For me, his story began over thirty years ago, when the barbarians crossed the frozen Rhine, weakening the already faltering West. Yet his career goes back even further to when these Vandals connected themselves with the Asian Alans, a nomadic people some 500 miles east of the Rhine, on the Danube River in Pannonia. Gaiseric was just one of many barbarian princes; nobody would have ever thought that he or his people could rise to a place where he'd become a threat to our Empire, however, he has carved out more territory out of our Empire than anyone in the history of Rome.

"What are your first memories of him?" Theodoric asked curiously.

"Well, first you should know that I was once a very famous tribune and, sometimes, I had the privilege of representing the even more famous commander, our great general Flavius Stilicho. However, back then, I was stationed in a garrison on the Rhine. Even then, the Empire was very threatened, although not as badly as today. Some of the lesser-known barbarians had already begun to trouble us back then. By that

I do not mean your people, young man, and you should know

that not all barbarians are equal.

"Which ones are the good ones?" Theodoric interrupted

naively.

Vitus had to smile at the young man showing his

inexperience yet again. He closed his eyes. "At that time, we

were allied with the Franks, a sturdy people high up in

Belgica, who were supposed to prevent other barbarian tribes

from crossing the Rhine, because from beyond that river, out

of the endless woods, new barbarian tribes kept appearing.

For centuries they've tried to invade our Empire again and

again. These are the enemies of Rome, and we will fight them

until the end of time. I was stationed up there with a small

force of *ripenses* to protect the border, and we paid the allied

Franks with gold to help us because that winter the Rhine was

frozen over solid and several barbarian tribes had already set

out to cross the Rhine into Roman and civilized Gaul.

At that time, I was still simply a centurion, stationed in

Mogontiacum. We were just a skeleton crew. A strong

*ripenses* that could really defend our borders had ceased to exist at that time. Troops were constantly being withdrawn and moved to other areas of the Empire. Then, at the same time, as I tried to organize a small defense before the first vanguards of the next barbarian migrants arrived, a huge Gothic army invaded Italy. Even General Stilicho could not defeat them in a single battle.

An army of 150,000 Goths plundered northern Italy under King Radagaisus, so Stilicho had withdrawn almost all the border troops from Gaul. He needed every man or it would have been the end of the West as we know it. And only with laborious blockages and division of the Gothic Army did Stilicho succeed and, eventually, he went in for the kill, and it is said that it was the slaughter of the century.

However, at first the Rhine was quiet but, further north, on the other side of the river, there was another a huge battle, but without us Romans present. Even before my time in Germania, the Franks had become our *foederati,* which meant they would secure the northern border of Gaul and, quid pro quo, were allowed to settle in the very north of Gaul. Even back then, it was already clear how weak our Empire had become. The older generations say that they never made peace with the barbarians. In former times, they would fight until the tribe was completely destroyed and only corpses and slaves were left. However, the barbarian tribes became ever more numerous, and individual tribes united to create larger ones. So, it was these Vandals who connected with the steppe-riders of the Alans, and combined, they were almost undefeatable.

Gaiseric was the bastard son of King Godigisel, the king of the Hasding Vandals, the eldest subtribe of this particular group of barbarians. They originally settled in the east where the forest gave way to the steppes, but they always had an urge to go west, so before they could devastate our provinces, General Stilicho made them an offer to settle north of the Alps. Honestly, he was anxious to incite the barbarians against each other and thereby reduce their numbers.

"Our renewed alliance with the Franks was meant to destroy the Vandals, and they almost succeeded. What the Franks didn't know, and what we Romans didn't know yet, was that the Vandals had united with the Asian Alans just before they had reached the Rhine, that they had combined their forces to form one huge army.

Prince Gaiseric, the youngest son of the Vandal king, was supposed to have helped the Alans king's daughter. These tribes had a pact and, together, they were too numerous and hard to beat. Nobody could stop them, and in the winter of the year 406 of the Lord, they stood at our barely guarded Rhine border. As far as I remember, this was probably the hardest winter I had ever seen, because the river was completely frozen over.

What was new and surprising for Gaiseric, however, was the fact that this King Merovee, the Frankish king, was not motivated by other tribes or out of need to attack the Vandals, but rather because his contract with us Romans obliged him to do so. Of course, we had to help with coins. Without gold, barbarians don't move.

The Franks were the border guards on the northern Rhine. Even then, we could no longer raise enough *ripenses* to secure the entire western border of the Empire, and Stilicho still had to deal with recurring Goth invasions in Italy. Our greatest opponent at that time was the Visigoth king and Eastern Roman officer Alaric, but that is a different story for another time."

Theodoric nodded in awe. "Sire, I need to know of how the other tribes fight – please?"

Vitus indulged in another goblet of wine, gesturing at the young man to be patient. "I will get to that. These huge hordes of Vandals and Alans, which Stilicho had tried to settle, had reached the Rhine that winter despite his best efforts, and that's when the Franks attacked the Vandals on our behalf. They had almost completed their slaughter when the Alan cavalry liberated them at the last minute preventing their complete destruction. So, the Franks fled back to their forests, but the Vandals and Alans gradually gathered again on the banks of the Rhine, ready to cross our border. We knew that if these mighty barbarian tribes really did dare to cross the river, then we would have no chance with so few men."

"Sire, I apologize," interrupted Theodoric, "but why were these barbarians all heading west at all?"

"Because in the east of the known world, live the deadliest of all barbarians, the Huns. Small, slit-eyed beasts who live on their horses. No one knows where they come from, but they have driven many of the other barbarian tribes to their doom. They also drove a part of your people, the Ostrogoths, across the Danube into the Balkans. All of this triggered a chain reaction, and the Vandals, as well as the Suebes and Alans, are a part of this reaction. The barbarians pushed unstoppably westward and, as I said, our great General Stilicho, who himself had Vandal blood in his veins and who could have beaten them all, even with so few troops, was occupied in Italy because the emperor needed him there.

"The barbarians had already committed small plundering and exploratory raids on our side of the river. Indeed, one morning in the late autumn during first snowfall, before the terrible winter set in, I saw from my watchtower a dozen small boats crossing the river. They went outside the garrison's city to the shore. I sounded the alarm, but we were maybe only thirty men strong at that point. We ran with our spears and shields through half the town before we came to a barn where the barbarians were just starting to steal our grain sacks. Somehow, the barbarians always knew exactly where to find what they wanted. But before we reached the barn, they saw us coming. They had gathered approximately twenty men, but they had no shields or armour, only axes, although a few men had swords as well. We moved in on them, slightly crouched, with spears thrust forward as we approached at a fast pace. We wanted to defeat them, with no dodging, no escapes. When the barbarians saw us, they came running and screaming toward us.

"We stopped right where we were, kept our ranks close together and waited for their attack with courage. 'Hold up your shields and stab into their bellies,' I ordered my men.

Like a thunderstorm, the barbarians all slammed against us at the same time. The impact was tremendous, and two of my men fell to the ground immediately. The barbarian axes smashed against the shields and hacked our men to pieces. They fought like crazed animals, trying to hit our heads – the preferred target of a barbarian. I fought with my men, shoulder-to-shoulder, fighting for my life again and again, their axes raining down upon us. But we were trained veterans. We shoved them away from us with our shields and continued to stab at them with our swords. Mostly we caught them in their ribs and legs.

I noticed a tall barbarian with dark hair and a terrible scar across his forehead. He fought skillfully; he was so agile and fast that we couldn't catch him properly. This was where I saw him for the first time, this young warrior who, it turned out later, was Prince Gaiseric. I remember he was one of the few barbarians who was armed with a sword. Finally, he stood right in front of me, raised his arm and with all his might hit with his longsword from the side and above. The blade crashed down and I heard a loud crash; my shield could deflect the blow but, in one move, I slammed into him with the edge of my shield and hit his leg, producing a bloody gash. The wound caught him off guard, and the man fell backwards. I was just about to follow up by piercing his neck when he jumped up like a grasshopper, turned and ran. But as he ran backwards, limping and bleeding, he gave a loud order and suddenly, as one, the barbarians turned around with the speed of lightning and ran like demons toward the riverbank.

I noticed that the young warrior with the sword had dropped something in his hasty flight. I picked it up and saw that it was a knife, a particularly thickly forged knife with a horn handle covered in carved runes. We watched the barbarians disappear into the snow-covered bushes, but this knife told me that this young man had to be a high-ranking warrior and leader.

At that point, we were too exhausted to take up the pursuit. From the cistern, I could still see the barbarians pulling sacks of grain out of the bushes onto their boats before they rowed back over the river.

We had beaten them that day, but we knew there was more trouble to come. Those little raids across the river had become more frequent and were just the prelude to a greater move. We knew from our scouts and barbarian spies that the Vandals were about to cross the river with their whole nation, just before the Frankish ambassadors arrived at our garrison to inform us that they were about to attack the Vandals. They said they were honoured to fulfil their obligations as *foederati*, but, of course, their visit was more about collecting Roman gold coins than fulfilling their duty. Nevertheless, the Franks must have smelled rich prey, as everyone is vulnerable when crossing a major barrier, and they knew Rome was a grateful buyer of slaves. They could capture the barbarians as they crossed and sell them to the Empire's wealthy citizens.

Moreover, the Vandals were too close to the territory of the Franks and that threatened their own territory. The Franks would attack, that much we knew, and so it came to pass. The Franks caught the Vandals as they set out to cross the river.

The battle was bloody, but the Vandal warriors were the better fighters. The Franks sent unexperienced, overambitious youngsters, and the Alan cavalry taught the Franks a lesson they will never forget. The Vandals even managed to catch the Frankish king, but they also lost their own king, Godigisel. It was the perfect outcome for us Romans."

"Sire, please tell me more of this Gaiseric?" demanded Theodoric, his eyes shining as he imagined the brave soldiers. "Did he fight the Franks too?"

"That's a rather long story, but it's important that you know that the year 406 was a crucial time for our Empire, because, after that, nothing was the same. The Franks ambushed the Hasding Vandals as they were crossing the Rhine alongside the cruel Suebes, who were sometimes allied with the Vandals but were often their enemy. Still, they are said to have made sacrifices for the Vandals as they destroyed what was left of the Franks.

After the battle between the Franks and Vandals, we bought some unfortunate slaves from the Vandals, whose warriors were still excited and shared the story of their success. Just the day before, Alan riders had arrived in the Vandal camp. They dragged Frankish prisoners behind them and among these half-slain creatures was the greatest prize the barbarians could ever have dreamed of – the Frankish king, Merovee.

However, I should mention that the Vandals were rescued by the Alans under King Respendial, who drove back the Franks. Otherwise, the battle probably would have been the end for the Vandals. A Frankish survivor appeared at my garrison after the battle and told me all of the bloody details.

A group of Alans dragged the Frankish king along. His tall figure was covered in blood. He had been on the verge of winning the battle and had felt like a sure winner because he had surrounded the Vandals. You must remember that the Franks are excellent axe throwers and skillful individual fighters. Only at the last minute did the unbelievable happen. The Alan riders appeared out of nowhere and covered the Franks with arrows. So a surprising onslaught from the Asians turned the battle, which was almost lost to the Vandals, to the point where the Frankish king had to abandon his fighters and flee. But the Alans caught up with the fleeing Franks, and the archers gave them no chance. The experienced Alan warriors also recognized the king among his few surviving riders. They surrounded the Franks who had no chance but to surrender or be killed on the spot. The Alans took them all prisoner, they knew that the allied Vandals would reward them generously for this beaten king.

King Merovee was thrown at the feet of the Vandal King Gunderic. This man wasn't very amused since their own King Godigisel had been struck by an axe while crossing the river. They said he drowned in the river but by his own blood, not water.

KingMerovee threw himself on the ground before the feet of King Gunderic, who could barely refrain from killing this old Frank on the spot. Gunderic couldn't wait to lay his hands on him, he called loudly to his riders: 'There he is, this dishonourable pig, whom each of us desires the ugliest death!' Gunderic put his feet onto to Frankish king's head. 'Now I have you there where you were always supposed to be. Stand up, worm, so I can see your traitor face better!'

He said it loud so that everyone could hear it. Some Vandal warriors who had lost their relatives to the Franks were on the verge of attacking him, but Prince Gaiseric held them back with a hand gesture and turned to his brother, Gunderic: 'If we kill him, he will be worthless.'

Gunderic looked at his brother in disbelief. 'I'll take care of this my way.' And he went back to the Frank. 'You know that you must die now. What you cannot imagine is how you're going to die.'

"Gunderic paused to let his words sink in, but the Frank showed no reaction. Gaiseric approached his brother and whispered something in his ear. Gunderic nodded grimly.

Then, Gunderic pulled on the king's beard. 'I'm offering you a chance to live if you answer my questions.'

Gaiseric moved closer. 'Speak up, dog, or we'll crucify you!'

'You can't do that, but there's still a king in front of you,' croaked the Frank, weak but still brave.

'And there is also one in front of you,' Gaiseric replied sharply, pointing to his brother.

King Merovee knew well enough what cruelties could be used to make someone die in agony. So, he consented to answer their questions and the Vandals learned how the Franks were paid by Stilicho to attack the Vandals in order to weaken both peoples against each other."

'Had no one suspected that this was Stilicho's plan? 'Theodoric asked hesitantly, scared he was insulting his new mentor.

'I had already thought at that time that this could be the case. After all, we tried to prevent the barbarians from crossing the Rhine border by all means. But at the same time, the Franks in Belgica grew stronger every year. Even then, Rome had to distribute promotional titles to the barbarians because of its own weakness. The Frankish king was questioned by Gunderic.'

'What do you know about the great river?' Gunderic asked. 'Is the way across the Rhine now clear?' he asked urgently.

The king nodded. 'In Mogontiacum, there are hardly any Roman soldiers left. We have a treaty with Rome to protect the border. No one can stop you now,' he replied.

Gunderic nodded slowly, but his evil grin didn't bode well. 'I'm giving your people a chance, but you have to pay for betraying us to the Romans.' Then, he called some barbarian officers to join him.

'The Alans will be rewarded by us, and your people will pay us plenty of Roman gold. Then, we'll leave just enough of your women and children alive so that your tribe will still exist.'

A short but cruel event followed. The king was bound, his right hand strapped onto a wooden block. It took a while, but then came a barbarian carrying in long pliers a glowing red-hot piece of iron. He pressed the iron into the hand of the Frank and began with force to strike a hammer on it. I've never heard such sounds from a human before. He hit the glowing blunt piece of metal with a hammer until the smoking hand was cut off. Then, the Alans were officially rewarded with a bag of Roman gold coins, and they removed the king. I gathered later that the king had died a few days later in the hands of the Alans.

However, Prince Gaiseric didn't stay long in the camp. He seemed to be angry. He moved with some groups, joined by the Alans, out into the hinterland of the Franks. They plundered their villages, spared no one, and razed most of their camps and huts to the ground. Afterwards, they offered us thousands of slaves. Most were young women and children, but there were too many of them for us to manage, and we had to turn most of them away.

The devastating defeat and death of their king quickly spread among the Franks. As soon as they saw the foreign riders appear, they fled into the woods, many in vain. Every day, Gaiseric returned to the camp with new spoils, such as cattle and weapons. He had confiscated everything, and what he couldn't move he had burnt.

Nevertheless, the Vandals had suffered casualties as well. They actually consisted of two peoples; the Hasding, the southern tribes of the Vandals, who were mostly warrior families and hunters, and then the eastern Silings, who were farmers and craftsmen. The Hasding had been hit by the battle hardest, and it took them many days to resume normal life. Like all barbarians, they buried their dead and even cared for their wounded until they were completely healed. They were accompanied by wound doctors who had the knowledge of how to treat injuries.

Gunderic, eldest son of the Vandal King Godigisel, took over the command of the Vandals and became King of the Hasding. In these times of need, however, it became clear how strong this barbarian tribe was. They hardly mourned their dead, and everyone immediately focused on where they were needed and the tasks that had to be completed."

# Chapter II

Vitus continued his tale, "A few weeks later, the time had come. On the last day of the year 406, the barbarians moved out of the woods, broke down their tents, and began to advance south of Mogontiacum to cross the now solidly frozen river,"

"So, all the Vandal people crossed this river and crossed the Empire's line," Theodoric surmised.

"Almost, with the Vandals and Alans, the Suebes people crossed the river further upstream near Argentoratum. Somewhere in the very far south, where the river was still narrow, the roughest barbarians, the tribe of the Burgundians crossed and went straight down to the inaccessible mountains, where they settled.

"We were far too few to do anything about it. We could not even try to block them. I saw how the first groups of several hundred had crossed the frozen river. It was a spectacle I could never forget. An unstoppable rabble was running through the landscape in dense rows like a worm. A huge barbarian mass with wagons, oxen, and family-gangs had invaded Gaul. We didn't have a chance of stopping them, especially not with the Alans and Suebes following right behind them. We had truly become a country without borders.

"We secured ourselves in our small garrison and hoped the barbarians would ignore us and move on. Of course, I sent out scouts with a couple of strong messages to the barbarians not to continue to move westward. Still, the border had become pointless. A few weeks later, we received General Stilicho's marching order to return to Italy by the spring.

"At that time, the barbarians had already penetrated deeply into Gaul, and the truth is that the barbarians were the greatest plague we Romans had experienced for centuries. Villages and towns were plundered, women were raped almost without exception, and then the villages were usually set on fire. They left a trail of destruction without reason. But Stilicho needed every man because we had to fight the Visigoths.

"So I was pulled out of my unit and reassigned to General Castinus. Castinus was the right hand of the magister militum, General Flavius Stilicho, and was in charge of large parts of the Western Roman army. It was a rather carefree time, as we were stationed in Northern Italy where, in contrast to Germania, nothing was lacking, and it was my task to replenish the troops. Yes, there were invasions, but the Roman army was spread all over, and unless you were directly engaged with enemy troops, you didn't notice that the Empire was actually on the brink of collapse. One thing I have to say about the state of our army at that time is that that our troops became, in a way, more and more barbaric. More and more foreigners were recruited, especially Gothic riders, and a strong cavalry mostly consisting of *foederati* was slowly replacing our traditional legions of foot soldiers."

"But why weren't there enough Romans to serve the Empire?"

"Smart question, young man. Being a soldier in the army had already become unpopular. The pay was rather bad and, above all, irregular, and it had become a risky career. Many locals hated the barbarians and word had got around that more and more of the officer positions went to them. It was true, even at that time, that many barbarian soldiers were given preferential treatment in Rome's service. And the old laws had become obsolete. The sons of rich Romans were, by law, virtually forbidden to become soldiers. It was a law that undoubtedly was created by the wealthy Senate, even though I must state that it was already law before I became a senator. See, Stilicho even allowed the Senate to make laws again! On the other hand, the Church offered a safe and often lucrative alternative to the dangerous and unpopular soldier's life. Many young people would rather be loyal to God and the Church than to a distant emperor about whom one had heard only bad things."

"So, the Vandals and Alans invaded Gaul everywhere and nobody was there to stop them?"

"That's how it was and, as I said, in the middle of winter I was ordered to Italy with the rest of the soldiers of my *ripenses*. Due to this most terrible winter, it felt like a death march for me. I reached Stilicho's camp near Ravenna around the first snow melt. At that time, the Empire was burning at every corner; the Visigoth invasions under king Alaric were hard to stop, and Stilicho needed all available troops, so even Gaul became secondary.

"It must have been 409 by then; I had been promoted to tribune, and we got the order to march in the direction of Western Gaul to confront the troops of the other emperor, the usurper Constantine, who pretended to rule the territory of Britain, Gaul, and Hispania.

"We, the soldiers of Castinus' troops, were loyal to young Emperor Honorius in Ravenna, and that's why Gaul was the battlefield of many parties back then, including those of the barbarians who for years had poured into the country like a flood of destruction, moving from the north on the Rhine and then slowly southward toward Hispania.

"And for all those years, the barbarians remained unchecked. We heard of the cruel fate of the people of Gaul, especially our veterans who lived out their pensions there as landowners. They were chased away by the barbarians, many were killed, and if they suspected anyone of having gold or weapons, they were tortured. We also heard that Stilicho was murdered by the emperor and that Rome, our eternal city, was plundered by Alaric and his Goths, who possessed the rank of a Roman general.

"Our troop was one of the first to leave Italy. We received simple orders directly from the emperor that we should go to south-western Gaul. In just one day, we had to pull out. After another difficult crossing of the Alps, it took us weeks to reach the city of Narbo. We suspected the troops of Constantine were north of it, but his army evaded us, and this gave our small army an opportunity to devote ourselves to a second task. Castinus, as well as us soldiers, wanted to stop the barbarians. We could not destroy them – for that, we were too few – but we could prevent them from reaching Hispania.

"As a true Roman, I wished for nothing more than to teach the barbarians a lesson. It was clear to me that they would murder all of us cruelly if we were defeated and captured, but I and most of the Romans in our army wanted their blood. For years, we had not been in a position to punish the barbarians. And here, near the sea and under the first foothills of the Pyrenees, I met them again.

"The Hasding had entrenched themselves behind an abandoned city, where the forest of the mountains began. Here, just behind Tolosa, we would finally be united with other Roman federations. Unfortunately, it didn't happen as planned.

"One morning, we were about to leave, when we received a message that foreign riders were approaching the unfortified town. Yes, our cavalry troop was battle-hardened, but we didn't want to risk our troops for barbarians. I asked Castinus to send me and a small troop of cavalrymen to chase the barbarians away. We thought they were waiting for us, and we gladly accepted the challenge, riding in the direction we suspected to find them.

"It was the late afternoon and drizzling, we weren't expecting a confrontation. Our scouts had just disappeared behind the hills when we noticed, from the opposite direction out of the forest, a small group of armed men moving towards us. But suddenly, the group swelled in size, so we quickly positioned ourselves on a hill, preparing for an attack. We placed our soldiers with shield and armour in the front line, behind them stood our archers, who tried to keep the barbarians at a distance. But the barbarians moved fast despite their suffered losses and, because they carried neither armour nor helmet, they moved in a zigzag course ever closer to our positions. I anticipated that we were going to be in hand-to-hand combat soon enough, but we were ready.

"The barbarians took cover behind bushes and ditches, then jumped up again, and seconds later, we were in close combat. Their battle cries were terrible. I stood right between the front soldiers and archers; our soldiers were, as expected, the better fighters, and we had superior weapons and armour. We kept the beasts off our backs as best we could. After only minutes, many barbarians were lying dead in the grass, struck by our arrows, so I expected them to stop at any moment and turn back and run as they often had before. But they fought on and on. The number of dead increased, and I wondered about their recklessness.

"Suddenly, dust clouds appeared to our right. I shouted to our soldiers: 'Horsemen!' The thundering of hooves became louder, and I recognized the troops and the small horses and

the riders with pointed helmets. Alans! I was worried because
I knew the Alans were allied with the Vandals and thought
that this was probably a trap.

"I soon realized that there had to be about a thousand riders
at least, far more than our legion numbered. We quickly
formed a half-circle, our back covered by a wooded
escarpment.

"But we had already been spotted by the mounted
barbarians. The riders managed to encircle us despite the
forest, which they rode through easily with their small horses.
We raised the eagle flags, the barbarians must have
recognized that we were only a vanguard and were, above all,
without baggage. This was exactly the situation the barbarians
preferred; we were prey for them. So, I lowered the standards,
signalled that we surrendered, and they halted as one.

"The Alans aimed their arrows and the Vandals pointed
their spears at us while we tossed our swords onto the grass.
We tried to communicate with them, and I personally handed
them a small sack of gold coins, trying to explain to their
leaders that we belonged to Emperor Honorius' troops and not

those of Constantine. The barbarians mumbled to each other, and I wondered if we would be taken as prisoners or just slaughtered where we stood. And, indeed, like a miracle they took the gold, turned away from us, and rode on! We couldn't believe it, but they knew exactly what they were doing because I realized to my dismay that they were riding toward our camp. So, as fast as we could, we rode after them at a safe distance. Of course, we were too late.

"I could see dust their dust in the distance. The Alans had already surrounded our main camp, and, although it was fortified with a small earth wall and makeshift palisades, I already knew that my men were as good as lost.

"Their riders shot my soldiers with hundreds of arrows; it seemed the sky was black with them. Some got off their horses and, almost unmolested, they filled the small earth ditch at several places with mud and wood at the same time. Yet again the riders shot their arrows at the soldiers, who could do nothing else but try to take cover behind the palisade.

"We rode at full speed towards the horde. I still don't know why I got involved with my few men, since they had just let us live, but I had to do my duty.

"It was unbelievable. Surprisingly, the riders opened their formation, and we stormed into emptiness. They looked at us in disbelief and made room. They rode away, then divided the riders, one group swinging to the left, the other to the right. They rode around us in large arcs as the circle closed behind us. The Asian bastards had us surrounded again! At the front of the palisades, I could still recognize how the hand-to-hand combat started. The shouting was unmistakable. Many barbarians had got off their horses and tried to climb over the palisades. Some of the riders were so good, they simply approached the fence at full gallop and jumped over it, something only the best of us could do. I saw how our men pressed the oval shields against the barbarian intruders. Yes, I must state that in close combat, we were usually superior to the Asian creatures. We stabbed them good – in the sides, in the face, in the testicles. We stabbed and stabbed. I only noticed screams and dust.

"Then, I looked at the horsemen around us. There were at least five hundred against our small group. We had placed ourselves in a circular defence as well as possible; overlapping shield to shield, we were expecting their final onslaught. I had to make a decision. Either we would all die right there on the spot or once again lower our arms. So, I gave the sign. Fortunately, our troops still kept their discipline, even in heavy combat. We lowered our swords and moved back a few feet so that the barbarians understood. That was the end of the battle, and a new beginning of my life in Gaul.

"I was captured and tied up. Hours later, I witnessed what I had feared. The legionnaires were bound and led away in long rows in different directions, each group awaiting its own fate. After that skirmish, we were, at most, a third of the original strength. The rest of our troop lay dead or dying in the dust, the barbarians acting as though they were not there.

"I stayed with the Alans for only a few nights along with a few other legionnaires. We were tied behind their horses and, after about four days of marching in the harshest conditions, with hardly any food and cold nights in open fields, we finally reached the Vandal camp. They were obviously working with the Alans. However, even I, the general of my troops, was ignored. In a simple tent, I waited with the soldiers who were under my command.

"On the third day, I was brought outside. Before me was a familiar figure. I recognized the tall barbarian, who carried a particularly long sword that day. He aimed his sword at my head. He was the same man who had escaped from me when they plundered on the Rhine. My men looked at me, fear in their eyes. I had to kneel in front of everyone. But I tried not to show my anxiety, it would have been bad for my soldiers' moral if I had. I had to assume that the tall barbarian didn't want to kill me, so I held still and looked straight into his cold, grey eyes.

"The barbarian said something that I didn't understand. A Gothic mercenary among my men offered to translate. I was been told that this was Prince Gaiseric, the brother of Gunderic, King of the Vandals. He said they just wanted to cross the mountain pass. The captured Romans would come with him as hostages, and we would stay alive. I was also told that some of my soldiers would have part of their foot chopped off as a warning to the rest of us not to run away. I looked at my soldiers sitting on the floor and tied up. They seemed to be frozen in place. They could not believe it. There was no escape from this situation, we had been lured into a trap and caught.

"I found courage and spoke up to the prince. I said we weren't in their peoples' way. We were on our way to the coast. 'But if you mutilate us, you are eternal enemies of Rome.' The prince said something, and suddenly, the Alans next to him stretched out their bows. I called for them to stop, raised my arms, and bowed before the barbarian prince. The Goth translated briefly that his patience was at an end and that I should speak quickly as to whether I could help them or not. I nodded and shouted out the names of some of my officers. I asked him to undo our shackles, and it happened immediately. Some of my men knew their way around Southern Gaul, so I explained to the barbarian prince that we would help them as long as nothing happened to us.

"The prince then gave us food, and our wounds were treated. The next day, we had to march again, mostly without food or breaks, and we were dragged to the foothills of the great mountains. There, we finally reached the main camp of the barbarians, a gigantic wagon circle, a typical laager, which was the home of a large part of the barbarian people.

"Despite everything, Gaiseric must have recognized me but I had no chance to speak to him for a while. After our arrival, we were fed generously, and gradually I regained my strength. So far, none of my men had been seriously harmed. Nevertheless, I absolutely had to speak to the barbarian prince. My Goth man passed on my request, and before the evening fell my gothic translator and I were escorted to the tent of the barbarian prince.

"I was allowed to sit across from him, and I thought I saw something close to a small smile on his hard face.

"He said, 'I recognized you even before our troops met. I need an experienced Roman officer to serve us Vandals. You're too important for me to make you a simple slave. Stay close to me as a messenger for various things and teach Latin to me and my most important men. Serve me well, and nothing will happen to your men.'

"When my soldier had finished translating, I was deeply shocked. I looked around at the murderous barbarian faces awaiting my answer. I nodded and bowed on my knees as I whispered: 'I recognized you as a prince before. We were fighting each other on the Rhine, and you lost a knife, a special knife decorated with runes. I have treasured that knife. If you spare our lives, I will be at your service.'

"He waved and I was taken away, but after that, everything changed. From then on, I was Vitus, teacher and prisoner of the barbarians."

"What about your men?" asked Theodoric, lost in his teacher's tale.

"They were dressed in Vandal clothing and had to perform countless small jobs, the type that women normally do in our country, but they could move around freely. Only one of them tried to escape, but they caught him and he was nailed to a tree. After that, no one dared to even attempt to flee. This barbarian prince had turned the tables on us – he was doing to us what we used to do to them."

"And you were always at the forefront of battles, as a Roman prisoner?" Theodoric asked in astonishment.

"Of course. I was not only his translator, but also his hostage for the moment, a reserve kept just in case. But over the next few years, I was never left unattended. Escape was unthinkable and, to be honest, after so many years I had become used to my not unpleasant surroundings. I was treated very well and, finally, the king rewarded me royally. I didn't want to leave either."

"What became of your comrades?" Theodoric asked.

"Well, what became of the prisoners of the Alans, I don't know. I suppose they were gradually sold to other barbarians or simply killed. But I can say that the legionnaires whom the Vandals held were gradually released over the years, mainly later in Hispania. General Castinus paid a good sum of gold coins for most of them, but not for me. Perhaps that was one more reason why I saw Castinus only as an incompetent, corrupt paymaster, who was no real Roman to me. Now, let me continue to tell you about the confrontation between we Romans and the barbarians.

"The barbarians had wreaked havoc in Gaul. They broke into every farm and took what they wanted. Grain and cattle were inevitably stolen. Slaves were captured, and many were sold back to us Romans. That's how they lived. I wondered why Rome could not send an army against them, at least in Gaul. But in hindsight, I must say this was a sign of the times. The barbarians became stronger, and Rome, it seemed to me, was at last approaching its sunset.

"In any case, the long trek of the barbarians, not only the Vandals but also the other tribes of the Suebes and Alans, went further south. Their goal was Hispania. There is where they wanted to settle. It felt more secure against potential attacks from the Romans.

"The first weeks marching toward the mountains were arduous. The barbarians tried to cross the Pyrenees, but many passes were too narrow, too high, and especially unsuitable for transporting cattle. There, in the mountains, lived even wilder barbarians than the Vandals. In addition, the Suebes tried to forestall the Vandals. They wanted to seize the best lands in Hispania. There was a strange kind of competition between the Vandals and Suebes. Sometimes, they worked together, but at other times they tried to annihilate each other. Overall, the mighty tribe of Goths threatened them both, because a gigantic Goth army was gradually coming over from Italy and moving toward southern Gaul, searching for land and living space along with the rest of their tribe.

"However, before the Vandals crossed the mountains, King Gunderic gave the order to plunder the most important city of Gaul, the barbarians had now reached Toulon. The city and small garrison units initially put up fierce resistance, but the huge number of barbarians and lack of support from Ravenna made any resistance ultimately futile. From outside the walls, I saw pitch-black smoke hanging over the city for days. For miles around, everything smelled like smoke and death.

"Finally, Gunderic gave the order to pull out. There was nothing left in this town to destroy. The barbarians had done a hugely successful job. The city was completely burned out. Whole houses had collapsed because their columns had been torn down; between rubble and ashes lay the slain, over whom disaster had come out of the blue like lightning.

"Gunderic had also found treasures, but they were things that only barbarians would appreciate, such as slaves, weapons and large herds of cattle. They even had some fine fabrics, but they were far from what Gaiseric and his people had hoped to find. Transportation turned out to be difficult as they had planned to cross the mountains, pulling everything they had on ox carts. They insisted on carrying everything with them because they believed that all of these treasures of Gaul would help them to found a state in their new homeland.

"After plundering and destroying the city, it took some time until the Vandals restored order in their ranks again, but then the march continued at a fast pace. They took the road to Narbo to find that the Alans hadn't left much of this city either. The Alan king, Respendial, had set up camp near Narbo, where he wanted to wait for the Vandals before crossing the passes. They took a few days of rest because the warriors were tired, but when they saw the Suebes approaching in the distance, they set off at once.

"The Roman road now led straight to the south. They left the lowlands of Narbo and slowly went uphill. In the distance, they could already see the wide slopes and summits of the mountains, which stubbornly guarded the border to Hispania. I caught Gaiseric's attention as I had some knowledge concerning the terrain and passes of the area. I actually showed him the most suitable pass: 'This is the way across the great mountains. Just one quick, steep climb. Then, we're in Hispania.'

"Gaiseric was seized by a feverish excitement as we drew closer to our goal. What could his people expect there? Was it really the land of their dreams where could they finally find peace and a place to live away from Roman threat? I could see these questions going through his mind as we followed the steeply ascending road.

Gaiseric looked critically up the pass. He recognized that a well-trained and armed troop could make this difficult pass invincible.

# Chapter III

Vitus restored himself with another goblet of wine and signaled to a nearby servant to fetch a new amphora. Theodoric waited impatiently for him to continue his account. "The cloud of dust in front of them suggested that there were many horsemen ahead of them. Gaiseric looked to the mountains, which were not very high at this point, but whose higher snow-covered peaks shone in the sun. From one of the valleys, we could see a train of wagons moving towards the Roman road. On the plain, another dust cloud appeared, but it was not caused by the wagons. The mystery was solved when we rounded the next hill. Gaiseric was pleased when we discovered that the Alans rode on the road before them and that the dusty train must be the Suebes many miles behind them. Gaiseric spurred on his horse and soon caught up with the slowly trotting Alans. King Respendial laughed when he saw Gaiseric.

"I guess we'll run into each other over and over again!' he shouted to him.

"Gaiseric replied just as jovially: 'You can't break away from us because you need us as much as we need you. Where do you come from with your men now?'

"Respendial became serious again. 'I believed there was a way through this large wide valley into the plains. We Alans need grassland for the horses.'

"'And what did you find?' Gaiseric asked amused, because he already knew what was coming.

"Respendial made an angry gesture. 'We found these lousy Suebes, who are right on our heels. Like us, they have followed this miserable little river in the hope of being on the right path. I'm beginning to think there's no decent passage through these canyons. We also had to cross the river at a narrow point,' he added resignedly.

"'Don't worry, there is a good passage, and it's not far.'

"'You know the way?" Respendial asked, surprised.

"'Yes, but my scouts have brought me some bad news to share with you. The lousy Suebes sit up at the pass with strong armed forces. They've already sent part of their army up there. They are probably well-armed. They want to keep

Hispania for themselves and deny us access to the pass and to the peninsula. The scouts say they have positioned themselves in such a way that we will suffer great losses and must turn back.'

"The Alan king was angry and almost turned red. 'They will not succeed. We Alans have a right to migrate.'

"'Let us meet tonight at Gunderic's tent and discuss everything. I believe that, for once, we can teach the Suebes a lesson.'

"With these words, he left behind a completely bewildered Respendial.

"The farm was built slightly uphill on a slope. From there, you could see the whole valley. But now it was dark, and a huge fire illuminated the area of their camp with its flickering glow and the night sky was strewn with stars.

"King Gunderic had transferred the leadership of the troops to his brother and war minister, Gaiseric, who looked down from his seat over the many small campfires where the other nobles sat and discussed the details of the forthcoming battle. It was a peaceful evening, and yet, everything was different.

The smell of the flesh sizzling over the fire could not distract from the fact that tomorrow they would have to fight a battle that would cost the lives of many men. It was not a matter of attacking a defenseless city but rather of fighting through the high forested pass, where there was a battle-tested army ready and possibly even supported by some Roman troops. The Suebes wanted to defend every inch of the ground and to make the Vandals flee."

"Perhaps that was a chance for you to flee as well," Theodoric suggested.

"It had actually crossed my mind to take advantage of the upcoming battle to flee to the Roman troops, if there really were Romans there. Unfortunately, it did not happen, and perhaps it was better that way.

"Nevertheless, all the captive men of my old legion knew that the next day there would be a decisive battle between two armies of barbarians. Serious and withdrawn, the warriors chewed on their pieces of meat. Gaiseric had ordered them to fill their bellies again so that the next morning, there would be nothing left. According to him, you could only hit your opponent with the relentless attack of a hungry wolf on an empty stomach.

"Most irritating was the Arian priest who went from tent to tent persuading the barbarians that they would go to heaven if they killed Catholic Christians should they encounter them.

"Gaiseric spoke to me about it. He asked what I believed. Could it really be God's will for people to slaughter each other just because they believed in Him differently? I said God treats all people the same. But he rightly suspected that the respective leaders of the faiths were bending God's will as they needed it. But just as the thought had come to him, it disappeared again. His goals were earthly in nature. He also encouraged the men, patting them on the shoulders and letting them know that he would rely on their invincible strength when the battle started. The warriors looked at him gratefully, and Gaiseric's trust in their power flowed through their bodies. Everyone knew from the meetings that it was Gaiseric's attack plan and that he would be the one to lead the attack. So, they were confident that they would win. He had the respect of all the warriors and stubbornly maintained the belief that the spirit of the great Gondensil had passed over to him and supported him with his wise advice.

"Surprisingly, King Gunderic had immediately agreed to Gaiseric's plan of and entrusted him with the leadership of the attack. Gunderic also approached Respendial and squeezed out an apology: 'Let's forget our old quarrels, Respendial. Alans and Vandals belong together, so let's fight together.'

"The Alan king remained cool: 'I have not changed my mind about a future distribution of land in Hispania, but for all of our interests, we must stick together. That's why I'm here.'

"Gunderic acknowledged this with a small smile and asked Respendial to take a seat in their circle. He sat down next to Gaiseric and gave him a brotherly pat on the shoulders.

"Then, Gaiseric stood up to address the nobles: 'May everything succeed as we have planned so that we can hold our swords up to heaven afterward.'

"The day of the battle began gloriously; blood red, the rays of the sun fought through the morning mist. The huge cavalry of the Vandals and Alans stood ready where the pass forked into a wide slope. The Suebes fighters took up their positions on each side of the pass.

"Gaiseric stood with Gunderic. Respendial looked around once more and checked the scene. It was an uplifting image to see this army from different peoples ready to fight together. All stood motionless on the spot and wondered why Gaiseric had not yet given the signal to attack.

"Suddenly, a Vandal in a Roman uniform rode down the slope. This made me think about how many foreign mercenaries served us Romans; many played double games. We Romans paid, armed and gave land to the barbarians, but in our hearts they had remained barbarians and were our eternal enemies.

"'You were right, my king,' said the soldier to Gaiseric. The Vandal spotted me, gave me a suspicious look, and continued talking to Gaiseric. 'The Suebes have mostly foot troops and only a few riders. However, they have sealed off the Narbo Valley, which means they have positioned themselves in front of and behind us. Also, the Suebes are well-armed with equipment they have received from the

Romans. However, they have only a few allied soldiers among them. We must fight bravely to get through.'

"'Roman units?' Gaiseric asked grimly.

"The warrior just shook his head, turned around, and rode off at a gallop. I still remember the incredulous look on that rider's face, as if he didn't believe that Gaiseric would ever succeed in breaking through the pass.

"Around noon, the Vandals gathered their auxiliary. They came through the bushes and hid in the forest, wanting to surprise the Suebes. Just ahead we could recognize the line-up of the Suebes. Somehow, they must have suspected that we were nearby.

"So far, the Suebes had remained in their positions. They did not move to challenge the Vandals. Directly from the forest, perhaps 60 paces away, their cavalry took their position facing toward us. Gunderic wanted to give the signal to attack, but his brother Gaiseric held him back, wildly gesticulating to wait for the last moment. But Gunderic was struggling to hold back; he leaned towards Gaiseric and said in a hushed tone, 'Look at these arrogant Suebes. They have good swords, but that's all! We attack immediately!' Gaiseric put a finger to his lips. He whispered because he had a plan that not all the warriors should hear.

"Unexpectedly, Suebes archers began to shoot into our lines. Fortunately, the Vandal shields held, but the barrage caused confusion, which Gaiseric had been trying to avoid.

"What could the barbarians do? Their archers couldn't hurt the Vandals much, but their attack seemed like a diversionary maneuver to distract the Vandals. I ducked deeper into the bush. It looked as if every enemy barbarian was staring in our direction. How did they know where our position was? We waited, hidden.

"Suddenly, Gaiseric ran through the dense trees and ordered every man to stay at his post and not attack. Then, suddenly, we heard screams. Behind me, shadows appeared in the deep bush, they turned out to be a massive number of warriors with oval and red-painted shields beating their way through the bushes. With their swords drawn, they attacked us from behind. It had been a trap!

"The first close combat began with swords clashing in the semi-darkness of the bushes. There in the forest, the Vandals were at a disadvantage with their long spears, so the Suebes pushed and pressed with their shields. More and more terrible screams rang out, and every barbarian fought like the devil. Still, I could recognize that more and more Suebes were coming from behind. They pushed us out into the open where the Suebes cavalry was waiting in the opposite forest on the other side of the field.

"I ducked and crouched, crawling deep into the bush, because if the Suebes caught me, at best I would die unarmed by a barbarian sword. At worst, they would make me a prisoner, and the Suebes were known to burn Roman prisoners alive. There was chaos all around me. I crawled ever deeper into the wood. Here and there, I saw the shadows of the fighters. The bushes and trees were now so dense that there were no tactical advantages on either side. Still, the Suebes pushed the Vandals slowly out of the forest and into the open.

"Then, strangely, I heard thunder. I looked through a clearing into the open field but saw only dust. Suddenly, a strong hand pulled me up by my arm. It was the prince himself. 'Get up!' Gaiseric yelled at me. 'You come with me and stay by my side.' He pushed me forward. Only a few meters around us, the stabbing and beating continued. I turned around and saw wild riders riding out of the cloud of dust towards the now-emerging Suebes cavalry, who rode out of the opposite woods. Then, I saw how the Suebes seemed to be wrapped in a black cloud of arrows.

"'Our Alans!' shouted Gaiseric. 'Forward into the open! Get out of the woods!' He pushed me into the open field, and there the confusion became complete. The barbarians were now all fighting in the open field, but the Alan cavalry had surrounded many Suebes who had been squeezed closer and closer together. They were dropping like dead flies as they were hit by arrows from behind. All the Suebes tried to flee now, but against the fast and better riders of the Alans, they stood no chance. The Suebes tried to escape up over the pass, but not many of them got far as the Vandals followed and threw their spears at their backs. I could see only clouds of dust and then, suddenly, there was silence. The Suebes were fleeing in all directions. The dust gradually thinned out and revealed the now-free pass. There was a moment of silence, and then a mighty hurrah sounded as Alans and Vandals together raised their weapons to the sky. The battle was over.

"We later found out that the Suebes had tried to block the pass not only for their own benefit but because the Emperor Honorius in Ravenna was said to have sent them equipment and many gold coins. The Roman opinions was that there should be as much barbarian blood spilt as possible on all sides to slow their advance. That was our strategy at that time, the methods of the emperor without clothes, so to speak. But that was not the end of the hostility between Vandals and Suebes. Soon, their paths would cross again. Barbarians loved to slaughter each other, but at other times they got along just fine. A typical characteristic of barbarians everywhere.

"Gaiseric, however, now urged haste. He absolutely wanted to return to the base camp as quickly as possible because there was a great danger that the usurper, Emperor

Constantine, for whom all barbarians still had ample respect, could attack from the rear while we still hadn't reached Hispania.

"The army finally moved on, fortunately without any of Constantine's troops showing up. Most of the passes had already been passed, and after many days of difficult riding we made camp at the foot of the mountains, now on the south side, near the pass road.

"We camped here for two days, and then the people of the Vandals and Alans were ready to leave. They crossed the last pass with their wagons, and it cost them a lot of effort and sweat. Gaiseric, after he had passed the last and highest point, had the soldiers make the road impassable with boulders so that any possible pursuers were blocked and had remove the stones before going onwards.

"The barbarians had finally reached Hispania, and so the two tribes struggled their way further and further south. When I looked back from the front of the column, it looked like an endless worm consisting of wagons, cattle, and a multitude of barbarian families. Even a number of escaped Roman slaves had followed. I could not see any Roman resistance, or any from the locals; they all fled as soon as the news came that the Vandals had arrived! Just before Tarraco, they managed to take a Roman fort. Completely surprised and unprepared, the Roman soldiers had no choice but to endure the onslaught. Gunderic proceeded as he always had done. First, he unleashed his military power so that their enemy's fighting spirit was quickly broken, and when the last of the resistance died, he gave the city to his fighters to plunder. Most cities followed this stratagem and, as always, without mercy and with vast destructive power."

"And help never came from Rome or from other Roman units?" Theodoric asked.

"Not at this point. It was not until they reached the grand city of Tarraco that the Romans found the time and strength for a serious resistance. However, the problem of the Roman inhabitants, as well as the soldiers in the garrisons, was that not all of them knew about the advance of the barbarians. It seemed that most of the connections to the heartland had already broken down. As far as we understood, even the supply of grain for the sparse garrisons had collapsed in these turbulent times.

"Emperor Honorius must have completely misjudged these barbarians, because this was a people looking for more than just living space. They wanted to conquer the land, and through the many fights over the years, they had become hard and merciless over their long journey. I must admit that my captor, and later friend, Gaiseric had changed over the years. Time and fighting had made the young, impetuous prince a strong, hard leader, respected by all of his men, for whom a human life counted only when it was useful to his people.

"As soon as we overran any Roman fortifications, all of the equipment and weapons were immediately collected for distribution among the barbarians. Quite often, the Romans had to be tricked into submission; the vanguard of the barbarians was often a Vandal dressed up as a Roman guard. That's how it worked in Juncaria. It took the barbarians only two days to turn it into a heap of rubble and ashes. With the city ablaze like a beacon, they announced that the Pax Romanum was now also over in Hispania.

"We followed the road to the coast, which was quite steep at first, but then, in more gentle turns, it led through the valley toward Tarraco. At a suitable place we set up camp again and drove the wagons together to construct the well-known fortifying laagers. We set up like this every night so we could resist attacks from any night attackers.

"The Vandals had arrived in the land of their dreams, but no one could have any real joy for this land was very different from what they had imagined. Personally, I thought things would get better after I earned my captors' trust, but Hispania was hell for everyone, not just for the prisoners.

"Hunger was my first and last thought every day. There, on the dry coast, there was neither suitable pasture land for cattle, nor could enough food be obtained from the impoverished cities. So, the barbarians wanted to go further west and south; they needed better living space and security, as well as enough food for the starving column.

"Yet again, the caravan went further south. Like a long snake, the barbarians crept through the valleys and plains further and further into Hispania. Another pass through rough terrain had now come into sight. Gaiseric, riding beside Gunderic, could clearly see hectic activity there.

"He waved me over to him. 'Did you know that Romans are stationed on the next pass?' he asked suspiciously. I denied knowing but said that I suspected it. It was obvious that every conceivable obstacle was guarded by a small cohort. 'They're trying to slow down your march, Sire.'

"He nodded. 'We will have to fight again, for the Romans up there are preparing to receive us.' Then, he used a gesture of his hand to indicate that I was no longer needed.

"But then, something completely unexpected happened.

"Roman riders rode down the pass towards us. There were only a handful of soldiers, and I recognized a centurion by his helmet. Gaiseric and Gunderic also recognized that these were ambassadors. So, we rode towards the delegation.

"The ambassadors didn't say much, but they gave Gunderic a scroll. Gaiseric presented the scroll to me for translation. I almost swallowed my tongue translating it. The Romans were actually offering the barbarians a contract for federation. None of the barbarians could contain their happiness and yet,

I thought, if the emperor was so weak to turn even the cruellest and most useless barbarian tribe into allies, then the Empire must be in a real crisis. I kept that thought to myself and translated the treaty precisely, including the terms that stipulated that the Vandals and Alans should separate and march back to Gaul again. Once completed, the Romans would then find land for them, and the contract would come into effect.

"Gunderic laughed and ordered me to write that the Vandals would like to be allies of Rome but couldn't be bothered with empty promises. Gaiseric also understood that the time was not yet ripe for such an agreement.

"The Alans also refused; they wanted to penetrate deep into Hispania and also free themselves from the annoying Suebes. Gaiseric and Gunderic were at loggerheads as to whether they should listen to the Alans at all. But the decision was made: the Vandals would march on and if the Romans decided to fight, they would accept battle.

"None of us knew then that there would soon be a repetition of the event, yet everyone knew that the Romans had, by no means, given in to defeat."

# Chapter IV

"Only later did I learn what was really going on with the emperor in Ravenna at that time. General Castinus was furious because he needed troops and the army master's permission to recruit reinforcements to beat the Vandals who had already crossed the border into Hispania. The new Magister Militia, who also commanded the most powerful of all Roman armies, refused and the senators preferred to negotiate with the barbarians so that they didn't need to contribute to the troops, while Honorius wanted to fight the Counter-Emperor Constantine. So, the high masters found common ground and decided to make the barbarians another offer.

"Castinus hit the table with his fist. That all had to stop now. He kept looking at the letter that the courier from the emperor's court in Ravenna had delivered to him and shook his head. He knew well enough that he could defend Tarraco with his troops. But he also knew that he had no power to destroy the barbarians completely or drive them out of the land. Now, the emperor himself ordered him to turn the barbarians into federalists. They should get the sparsely populated areas in the hope that they would then live in peace, but Castinus did not believe in it. Sadly, he looked out the window. A special courier had also brought the latest news from home, saying that some strange things had happened.

"The Goth Alaric had, after he had plundered Rome, moved further south but failed miserably in his attempt to cross over to Africa. Many of his ships had sunk in a storm, so Alaric had to cancel the crossing. Soon after, he died of a mysterious disease.

"His successor, Athaulf, married the sister of the Emperor Honorius, Galla Placidia, and moved further north with his Goths. It was rumored that Emperor Honorius had also promised him land in Hispania. Castinus had to laugh despite his anger.

"'Then, they will slaughter each other,' he thought maliciously; In the blink of an eye, he realized the strategy of the high gentlemen in Ravenna. They wanted to lull the Vandals into safety so they could bide their time until their arch-enemies, the Goths, arrived in the land. Until then, the Goths had always been the strongest of all the barbarians. But a fight with the Vandals would also weaken them because they would be not only dealing with the Vandals but also the Alans and Suebes. Castinus nodded his head. The emperor wanted to get rid of the Goths in Italy and, here in faraway Hispania, they would smash each other's barbarian skulls in.

"And so Castinus was ordered to Ravenna. Just before that, he advised that all the barbarians should be offered federation status at the same time, with the prospect that they would actually be allowed to settle in Hispania, but the Emperor in Ravenna waved this idea away. 'First, we want to strike them back. If our troops are not successful, we invite them for negotiation. In any case, we must weaken them beforehand.' He waved Castinus to a map. 'Here, across this river. If they want to go further south, they have to pass the city of Tarraco. Here, we will beat them. Do you understand your responsibilities, General Castinus?'

"'Here, we will not only hold; here, the Empire will strike back,' the devious general replied dryly.

"So, Castinus came directly over the sea and led his troops ashore in Tarraco. He couldn't gather much of a cavalry but received some strong units of the newly promoted Goths, all experienced warriors, who had the reputation of being some of the best warriors of the *foderati*.

"The Romans had entrenched themselves in Tarraco, and Castinus had declared the city a red line; he had the palisades restored as well as he could in a short period of time. But what he really had in mind was to finally engage the barbarians in an open pitch battle. Since crossing the Rhine in Germania, no real Roman army had been able to oppose them. The time had come for Rome to wipe those barbarians off the map.

"As always, the Romans proceeded very systematically. In the run-up they tried to weaken the barbarians as best they could. All the supply roads were filled with Gothic auxiliary, and every farm within 100 miles was set on fire. Whenever they could, the Romans tried to pick the battlefield.

"Before Tarraco, the terrain became mountainous again. And as if we had guessed all this, the Romans wanted to steer the Vandals into a pass on the narrow plateau. General

Castinus was a corrupt pedant; I knew that, but I also knew that he understood his craft as a general.

"So, if the barbarians wanted to go further south, they had to pass Tarraco and the plateau, which was not as high as in the Pyrenees but the terrain still offered enough difficulties to overcome.

"The blockade Flavius Castinus had set up against King Gunderic and his confederation with the Alans, had worked out perfectly until now. Hunger had made the tribes sluggish and had slowed them down; they were always in search for supplies.

"The vanguard I was riding with moved quickly. On the left, a lavish forest rested on the slope of the mountains. The woods seemed to me like a silent shadow, growing where we Romans used to farm. It seemed to be returning the Empire to the wild farm by farm, a beauty to behold. But for me, seeing these old abandoned borderlands was a sign of disaster. Behind us, on our right and in front of us, right to the mountain pass in the distance, was a vast, green plain. This kind of location easily explained why Hispania was a great land to raise horses.

"I was finally able to understand the problem the Vandals were facing after we left the valley. Around the vast plains of greenish hills, cloudy mountains and high, narrow passes surrounded the entire region. Castinus just had to take control of the various narrow paths between the valleys in order to box the Vandals in. They would be trapped with no resources. Nature often provided the Roman armies with a difficult terrain to slow their enemies down and with 'natural checkpoints' to control them.

"The Vandals were aware of this and they planned to take control of one of these obstacles, and the initiative that came with it. We passed terrain where the forest became more and more wild, only to abruptly subside when we reached the rocky, final path to the pass that impeded our travel to the city of Tarraco.

"I was always stunned by the huge number of riders fielded by the tribes. While light in its nature, the Vandal cavalry was swift and aggressive, far from a mere skirmishing force, leaving that role to the Alan horse archers. The Vandals were Germanic people and the Alans came from the Asian steppes. The two peoples shared little cultural connection when they first met but were now able to combine their different types of forces with more efficiency. Even among the Vandals themselves, unity was a new concept. Those riding to battle that day were mainly Hasding, who thought of themselves as the best and most fierce warriors among the confederation, but, of course, any of the innumerable different sub-tribes would have argued that point.

"We finally reached the pass where the Roman army was waiting for us. Contesting the pass was a good idea, what any capable general would do, but from my perspective, it was not clear if the Roman effort would pay off or whether the warriors of the confederation would prevail.

"A small palisade was built on the highest point of the rocky pass, and a line of red, oval shields was assembled in front of it, only four ranks deep, with archers, *sagittarii*, waiting to begin their volleys right behind them. Almost every single noble was wearing chainmail, a cheaper and inferior option compared to the metal strips of the traditional *lorica segmentata*. An officer, the vicarius, was screaming orders, pushing his soldiers to move forward. He was trying to move them into a wedge formation. At least, that's what I would have done to defend against the incoming cavalry, but he was having little luck convincing his men to follow orders. Those men were auxilia, less trained and capable by design, and they were green even by auxilia standards, a delaying force left to leave the real army enough time to prepare.

"Even hardened professionals were rarely ready to sacrifice themselves, so it was a miracle that these boys were still there to fight at all. On the right side of the Roman formation, a group of Visigoths riders, bearded and heavily armed veterans, were surveying the situation. I focused my attention on one of the banners on the palisade. One of them was familiar to me. Castinus, the general leading this whole war on the Roman side, was here, but I wasn't able to find his helmet among the ranks or behind them.

"Volleys were flying soon. I held the reins of my horse and broke off from the main Vandal unit, side by side with my keeper. A couple of stray arrows landed around us, very real proof of how close we were to the enemy. Both sides were exchanging projectiles soon, including arrows, light javelins and *plumbatae*, especially nasty darts thrown by the scared spear wielding auxilia. The Vandals left most of the projectile exchange to the Alans while they waited, like a pack of feral dogs, for a sign of weakness. On the right, a group of heavily armored Vandals positioned themselves in front of the Visigoths, screaming insults, challenging them, with their opponents answering in kind. Many among these elite Vandals were shining under the sun in their lamellae armor, small iron scales that made them look like bearded, lethal metal statues.

"The Roman center, under a terrifying barrage and the constant threat of the cavalry, slowly lost courage. I finally saw Castinus, appearing from behind the palisade to scream encouragement at his troops. He was accompanied by a couple of riders, dressed in heavy armor, with a red crest decorating the top of his helmet. The Vandals waited, ready for a charge that might come at any time. They were smelling blood, patiently waiting for openings in the Roman formation, for fear to finally break their enemies.

"There was nothing the vicarius could do and the tribunus, the commanding officer of the unit, was nowhere to be seen. The spear front bent at the center, creating small cracks in the shield wall, preliminary signs of the line disintegrating into smaller, separated groups fighting to survive. In unison, a terrifying war cry exploded from the Vandal ranks, signaling the charge. The first contact between the two forces was going to be the last.

"The bloody spectacle of a fight is something that I wasn't ready to pass up, not after months and months of boring marches. I rode closer to watch the events unfold. The Vandal riders streamed through the formation, avoiding direct impact at first. Some moved close enough to swing their sword down, hitting shields with sickening sounds. Spears kept thrusting, sometimes hitting metal armor that screamed against the metal, sometimes catching unguarded flesh. I looked on as the leg of a barbarian turned into a bloody crater, enough to make him lose his grip on his horse and crash down to the ground.

"The real charge came a few seconds later. The first Vandals had avoided direct contact, but the second wave didn't. Horses pushed the shields apart from each other, while the riders broke their spears mostly in the first blow, switching to axe and sword immediately after and raining down hit after hit. The Romans were pushed straight onto the riders surrounding them, moving inside the openings of their formations. But then there was no more room to maneuver. No escape. Many among the Vandals were dismounting now, screaming insults and war cries.

"I searched again for Flavius Castinus and saw him turning his horse and riding away. Of course, there was no reason for a general to die on that pass, but I couldn't help feeling betrayed as he abandoned those young boys to their deaths. The Romans knew better than to sacrifice themselves plunging into carnage. Their fight against their Vandal counterparts was clean, rank after rank hitting each other, passing through. They knew they were going to ride away alive. The Romans were a delaying force, and their death would have served their allies in the same way.

"Slowly, the riders of the Vandals and Alans formed up again. They gathered their foot troops and retrieved their wounded and dead from the battlefield. The wounded of the opponents were carried to the afterlife with targeted sword blows without mercy.

"Gaiseric nodded to me in passing and, in good Latin, said, 'Woe to the defeated.' That was our saying for 600 years!

"As I learned weeks later, however, there was one more epilogue. Roman envoys appeared in our camp. Somehow, our Roman troops had found out that the Vandals were holding a considerable number of Roman hostages. Gold coins were exchanged for Romans. Whether friend or foe, more armies could be moved with gold coins than by any other means. But as I feared, I wasn't supposed to be on the list of hostages."

"Maybe Gaiseric wanted to keep you," interrupted Theodoric.

"Well, I believe that in retrospect. But since those days, I've despised Castinus. In any case, the day after the battle, Gaiseric ordered me to join him in his tent. He offered me a cup of wine and got right to the point. 'As it is evident from General Castinus' offer, you weren't worth being freed.' I nodded, 'You are right about that, my Lord. He did not feel the need to help an old comrade.'

"'So, you have been a guest for a long time,' growled Gaiseric. 'I'll make you an offer.'

"I was bursting with curiosity. 'I'll hear it gladly, what do you suggest?'

"'You stay with us. You continue to teach Latin to my men and show us the details of how Romans fight. I'll pay you in gold, but I need your word that you will be loyal to me. If you don't want that, we'll ask this Castinus what he'd be willing to pay for you.'

"I felt the sun rise in my head. 'I accept your offer. I don't want to go back to Castinus' army.'

"Gaiseric grinned at me viciously. 'Who wants to be on the side of the losers?' He waved to a soldier who was preparing fresh barbarian clothes for me.

"Gaiseric again took command of the Vandal Army. Somehow, he was boiling with excitement. This great victory would only increase Gaiseric's popularity among his people. He had already agreed with Respendial that they would now take the cities of Julia Biterra and Agathe, which were practically without protection. The temptation to take rich spoils without having to fear great losses was too great. Even Gaiseric agreed, because it was not a long detour. And doing so got rid of a danger in their back when they had to fight their way into Hispania.

"The death sentence was passed on these cities, and the barbarians shared them among themselves. The Alans took Agathe and Gunderic took the rest.

"Again, the armies were set in motion. But this time, they went their separate ways. They all knew the war wasn't over yet, and the warriors' bloodlust hadn't been sated yet. Even if their own losses were small, some of them had been caught. Good friends, acquaintances and relatives had to be avenged. So, the disaster came upon these ancient Roman cities like a pack of wolves to a herd of sheep."

# Chapter V

"It was only a few weeks after the battle, and the Romans were all again at sea; some units even fled to Gaul. Most of the group was already far south of Tarraco, when one evening, a small troop of Romans rode toward us, surprisingly with lowered standards. I learned it was Castinus again, but thought that it couldn't mean what I imagined.

"The following morning, I learned the full truth. Gaiseric gave me the papyrus roll to translate loudly for him and King Gunderic. Castinus had proposed to offer federal contracts to all barbarian tribes. The kings and Castinus would meet at a common place, and Gaiseric would guarantee security. Castinus proposed Tarraco as the meeting point.

"The Hasdings, Silings, Alans, and Suebes, were to meet with the Romans under Castinus, expecting an advantageous trade with Rome. And, although Tarraco was in the hands of the Vandals, King Gunderic allowed the Romans to stay there as if the recent Roman defeat under Castinus had never happened. King Gunderic was, at first, not amused at all by their behavior and arrogance. Castinus had even dared to accommodate himself in the best villa, but unfortunately, King Gunderic found this out too late.

"The Vandal leadership gathered that evening, preparing themselves and anxiously awaiting the Roman legation for the first meeting. I was also invited to attend.

"As soon as the first Roman ambassador entered the hall of the forum, Gunderic burst out, 'If, at my next meeting, a Roman soldier does not bow before me properly, I will cut his head off and throw his carcass to the dogs!'

"An outrageous commotion followed. The barbarians insulted the Romans, and it almost looked as if blood would flow again at any moment.

"Gaiseric nodded to me to speak. Soothingly, I raised my hands, 'I'd at least like to hear what Castinus has to say. It might be quite interesting, so let us listen to him.'

"Gunderic made a throw-away hand gesture, meaning that his outburst of rage shouldn't be taken seriously. 'Bring in the ambassadors,' he rumbled in a much calmer tone.

"The messengers entered, and one could clearly see that they did not feel comfortable in their position. Again, they came right to the point. One of them read the offer and announced that in the next few days, as soon as the Alans and Suebes envoys arrived, decisions should be made as to what land in Hispania would be allocated to which people. Castinus would have the authority of the Emperor himself. In return, an agreement had to be signed obliging the tribes to send troops to Rome in the event of war. Thereby, they would actually become federates of Rome.

"I had just finished the translation when the delegates set about leaving the hall without waiting for an answer. Gunderic, so angry just moments before, stared speechlessly after them. After he had recovered from this surprise, he turned to me at a complete loss. 'What the hell was that?' he asked.

"I nodded with a smile, and his whole face radiated satisfaction. I explained, 'They have finally understood that they can no longer expel the Vandals from this country. That's why they're offering peace. They are so weak that they see no other way out to save what still can be saved.'

"Gaiseric got up. He realized what a chance they had in front of them now. He could offer his people a home and find peace for the time being. What would happen later, when they felt strength and a sense enterprise again, would be a different matter. He only thought of that briefly but kept it to himself.

"The same evening, all the chiefs and princes came together to vote on whether Castinus' offer should be accepted. 'So, who is against this idea of bowing to the Romans and moving into the assigned territories as federates of Rome?' Gunderic asked, looking closely at the line of his princes.

"Nobody moved. For a moment, it was as silent as a grave. Gunderic's voice thundered again: 'I can hear no dissenting voice! That's how it's supposed to happen! I will go to Castinus and make peace with the Romans.'

"'Provided the Alans and Suebes join in,' Gaiseric said warningly.

"'The Alans do nothing else without us. And the Suebes have no choice if we and the Alans stick together. Well, we agree!'

"The assembly responded to these words in a jubilant storm. At last, they could hope that their long journey had come to an end.

"Gaiseric gesticulated for quiet so that he could address the crowd. 'If the Romans want to provide land for each tribe, it can only be advantageous if the Vandals appear as two peoples, as Hasdings and Silings. Besides, my father already knew that this band of tribes would only last for the duration of the journey. Sooner or later, they would have parted anyway. I am much more worried about the fact that the Romans are making us such an offer without demanding anything in return.'

"The prince of Silings replied reassuringly: 'They want peace from us because they are not strong enough to drive us out of Hispaina.'

"Gaiseric nodded, 'I still see it that way, but my gut tells me that there's a catch, and I'll find it, I promise.'

"A nervous tension lay over Tarraco. In front of the gates of the city, the barbarian tribes of the Suebes and Alans marched into the city. Castinus only had a small team in and around the city to protect him if the barbarians attacked. But that wouldn't be enough if the Roman really aroused Gunderic's anger. Nobody trusted anyone yet.

"Castinus had determined that only a dozen emissaries per people should be allowed into the Principa Villa at sunrise. In addition, markings were placed on the square of the villa showing the emissaries where to line up. Castinus had filled an amphora with fine sand for the draw. After his observers had informed him that they were now suddenly four barbarian tribes, he had four stones of the same shape and size carved with the names of the provinces, mixed under the sand in the amphora. Since he had to assign only three provinces, the largest one had to be assigned twice. So, there was one stone each for the Baetica and Lusitania in the amphora, while Galicia was represented twice.

"Castinus sat at his desk and looked out of the window at the sea. Despite the calming view, he felt nervous. He took a deep breath. Today would be a day of great importance for the Empire and, by tonight, Hispania would never be the same.

"The fanfare started and gave the signal to open the gates of the inner city. Gunderic looked around uneasily as they rode through the streets of the city. On both sides, there were Roman soldiers lining the way to the meeting. There were enough Romans to make Gunderic nervous. He looked around for Gaiseric, who also watched every move the Romans made. 'I hope we're not walking into a trap here.'

"Gaiseric nodded to him comfortingly. He now understood enough Latin enough to understand the Romans. The way he saw it, the orders from Ravenna were clear, and Castinus wouldn't dare to break them. Their path ended in the big square in front of the villa.

"Behind them followed King Respendial with the Alans, whose wild and strange appearance brought the now-numerous population to fearful proclamations. Behind them came the Suebes, with King Hermeric at the head. Prince Fredebal of the Silings deliberately formed the end with his people to set himself apart from the other Vandals. They all formed a line now, as they had been briefed. In the meantime, the sun had risen so high in its orbit that it illuminated all of the square with its glistening light. The heat caused everyone's forehead to break out in sweat.

"But it wasn't the heat that made Gunderic feel uneasy. 'I can smell the scam already,' he whispered to Gaiseric, who nodded in agreement.

"But his dark thoughts were then distracted. General Castinus stood on a podium that had been specially erected for the occasion. The Roman fanfare sounded across the square. Then, dead silence returned. Castinus raised his voice.

"'I see you've responded to the Empire's call. Our Emperor, who rules and loves everything and every subject, has decided to take you into the womb of the Empire. In his unfathomable goodness, he wants to forget your hostile actions against Rome. He offers you territory here in Hispania if you agree to never again turn your swords against Rome. So that none of you can feel disadvantaged, a judgment of God will decide here and now where you may settle in the future. The decision is binding and cannot be reversed. The leaders of the individual tribes must now step forward to recognize these conditions.'

"Castinus took a deep breath after that speech. Now came the decisive moment which, in his opinion, would significantly influence the history of this part of the Roman Empire.

"Gunderic hesitantly moved forward with his horse. He solemnly raised his right arm and called out to the crowd: 'The Hasdings have never wanted anything other than a place for their people. So, if the trade is honest, we'll meet the conditions.'

"Respendial followed suit: 'The same is true of my people.'

"The Suebes with Hermeric, and the Silings with Fredebal expressed their agreement by also stepping out and raising their right hand.

"Castinus registered the reactions of the barbarians with satisfaction and gave the agreed sign. The fanfares started again, and from the staircase of the villa appeared two lightly dressed girls with the amphora and their important content.

"Castinus' voice resounded as he pointed to the amphora. 'In this vessel, there is a stone for each people on which the name of your future homeland is written. Step out one after the other and pick a stone out of the sand in the amphora. When you have it, hold it open in your hand so that I can see it. Then, I will proclaim loudly and clearly what is written on the stone, and my word will be law.'

"The leaders of the tribes dismounted from their horses. Breathless tension lay over the assembly. Gaiseric looked around for me, where I stayed in the background so as not to be recognized by Castinus. He knew which provinces were to be raffled. There was Galicia, which they already knew, and Lusitania far to the west, a country with long coastlines to the sea without return. But the best lot would be Baetica, according to Gaiseric. 'There, the sun always shines, and the land is fertile. God made a special effort in the creation of the Baetica.' Even the Romans raved about it.

"Gaiseric had high hopes. He said that the fertile fields in the lowlands of the estuaries on the coast would benefit his people. There, in the south, it never really became winter. The sea, with its abundance of fish, would help to feed the people, so they would never have to worry about food again.

"Now, everyone stared spellbound as Gunderic approached the girls with the amphora. Gaiseric whispered to me, 'Galicia would be a mistake. If it comes to that …'

"Gunderic stood before the vessel. He was the first to choose. Excited, he reached in and felt nothing but sand for a moment. He dug deeper with his fingers and then, felt a stone. He grabbed it tightly. As agreed, he raised his arm and opened his hand. Now, the stone was clearly visible in his palm.

"Respendial and Hermeric followed his lead. Fredebal was the last one who had to dig around in the sand until he found the last stone. When he finally had it laying in the flat of his hand, he trembled so much that he almost fell down with excitement.

"Flavius Castinus came up to them and looked at the stones they held. Almost with pleasure, he looked at these barbarian lords, who now stood here in front of him with their stones in the air.

"The tense silence tore at the nerves of those present, and Castinus took his time with the announcement. Then, he stopped before King Hermeric of the Suebes and shouted out loud and clear: 'Galicia II!'

"Hermeric flinched, and a disappointed murmur rippled through the ranks of his warriors. Castinus now stopped in front of Respendial, looked at the stone, and again his voice roared: 'Lusitania!' One could see how Respendial's soul jumped into heaven, and restrained joy spread among his people.

Now, it was the turn of the Siling leader, Fredebal. 'Baetica!' announced the insensitive voice of Castinus, and the cries of joy from the Silings echoed across the square.

"Gunderic's face paled. Angrily, his face distorted, and he didn't even wait until Castinus came to him. He took his arm down and stared at the stone. 'Galicia I' was carved into it. He felt an enormous heat creeping up his neck. He could hardly contain his rage. Even Gaiseric almost blacked out. They had traveled the longest way, and their best people had died to get here, only for this miserable land, which they now also had to share with the Suebes.

"To the solemn sounds of the fanfares, the federal treaties had to be signed by all, some with joyful hearts while others clenched their fists and entertained sinister plans in their minds.

# Chapter VI

Vitus paused, he seemed to be looking into the past as he recounted his tale. Theodoric tried not to fidget on his stool, though he was impatient to hear the rest. "Gaiseric, the Hasding prince, moved to the hidden villages with his small army, surrounding the valley of the mighty Ebro River.

"From here he made expeditions inland, getting to know the bigger cities such as Caesarea and Toledo in the south of the peninsula, and visited the legion camps of the Romans. Above all, however, a deep love for the sea developed within him, which never left him. Furthermore, he encountered more and more people, mostly merchants and settlers from beyond the sea, these were Berbers from North Africa. Gaiseric recognized their value as experienced seamen. Many also knew the foreign coastlines and were well informed about the strengths of the Roman garrisons in Africa. One particular merchant, by the name of Aniba, was hired by Gaiseric himself to show him how to steer a ship, find his way on the sea by using the stars and how to use wind and sails to set off. The prince and his chiefs often sailed along the long coast visiting the great ports of Tarraco, Barcino, Cartagena. For the barbarians, as well as for myself, it was a carefree time of learning and peace.

"Here I got to know Gaiseric more and more intimately. One evening he summoned me to his tent. Surprisingly, there were also women inside. Without question the large stocky woman wearing coarse cotton tunic and trousers was his wife. She brought a huge jug of mead – that's a fermented wheat water that, when you drink a lot of it, has the same effect as our wine. The barbarians sweetened this brew with honey and drank huge quantities of it every day. But it felt good. That night, I was drinking with Gaiseric and his wife, when the tent opened and a young girl entered. Gaiseric's wife began to speak in her low husky voice, 'This girl is a high princess and our niece, Hilda. We want you to marry her.'

"I was shocked and asked them why they wanted this.

"Gaiseric's wife smiled, her smile lit up her normally coarse face. 'You will not be our guest forever. You're important in Rome and we need influence there.'

"I asked what would happen if I refused.

"'Nothing will happen to you,' Gaiseric replied grumpily. 'You will continue to stay with us, we have plans to move on. You will continue to be my translator.'

"'But you have to try,' his wife insisted. 'Take the girl into your tent and see.'

"Gaiseric nodded to me, and I understood that this was an offer I shouldn't refuse. So, I took the shy girl by the hand and did what I was told. Fortunately, a marriage never materialized and I wasn't asked about it again. What still amazes me looking back is how much influence women have on the barbarians. It had become clear to me that Gaiseric's wife was anything but a passive housewife. Many barbarians listen to their wives with complete seriousness, a practice quite different from us Romans. I even believe that barbarian men do exactly what their wives tell them. They are often their secret advisors, listening and observing everything around them and later advising their husbands in private. I can also confirm this from my experience with the beautiful Hilda. She was my lover as well as a valuable counsellor until my return from Carthage.

"Otherwise, barbarian life was rough, at least the years in Hispania.

# Chapter VII

"I can say much about the wild Hasding Vandals and Alans, these tribes had been exposed to Roman civilization for centuries. However, even the peasant Silings were, from my point of view, still primitive. They were not stupid, but they hadn't been able to appreciate the benefits of civilization, some were even proud of their primitive ways. Anyway, those sunny days in Hispania, the plundered luxury that many barbarians had made their home, were not to last long for there was a lot going on in Ravena.

"Castius, just like any other Roman general, had not enough troops to wipe out these barbarian tribes completely. I mean, killing all of them down to the last barbarian, that's exactly how we delt with those folks for centuries. Once, in earlier times, when Rome fought an enemy then the fighting continued until the last hut was burned down or the last surviving barbarian had been made a slave.

"Of course, we had high hopes of our time-proven legions and commanders. But even the senators and Cesar himself realized that the Visigoths were too numerous to defeat or push them into far away provinces. The idea of giving land was an old one, so it was decided that we would give land within the Empire to the Goths, but they had to do us a favor in return. In the year 416 a good opportunity arose, so we sent the Goths to Hispania with the promise of receiving their own land."

"Were you going to use them against the Huns as well, Sire?"

"The Huns? Oh no, they couldn't be played like that, they are not even interested in land. Emperor Honorius wanted to use the numerically superior Goths to wipe out the Vandals, starting by weakening their under-tribe family, the Silings."

"How did he achieve it?"

"Fortunately for him, the Visigoth had a strong and ruthless king, Wallia, who did exactly what he wanted. They desperately needed land as well, but first they had to make an agreement with us, which included destroying the Vandals. So, the emperor incited the Goths against the Vandals, we even equipped them with weapons and ships to reach the

Vandals' territories faster. In the very south of Hispania, they went ashore and reached the rural area where the peaceful and Siling Vandals lived. Eventually they attacked, like wolves on unsuspecting sheep. Gaiseric himself told me the story of the survivors.

"The Gothic army bypassed the snow-capped mountains, even in the hot season they are white and cold, and crossed the plateau off Hispalis. Their army made rapid progress on the well-developed Roman roads. Their destination was the settlement area of the Silings, in the south of the Baetica, a fertile coastal strip where they thought they were safe.

"King Wallia led the army himself, constantly driving his chiefs to increase the speed of their advance. Since Wallia had seized power, the troops had been ruled with an iron fist. He was feared purely because he exercised his rule unpredictably and often cruelly. If anyone drew his displeasure, he was as good as dead. Wallia had his predecessor, Sigeric, killed so he could declare himself the new King of the Visigoths. He only surrounded himself with warriors who had fought with him in Radagaisus' huge army years before. This made him safe from anyone who secretly dreamed of seizing power in the same way as Wallia. He had managed to unite the Visigoths, who until then had been divided over old tribal feuds, and made them submissive to his will. He had not only succeeded using despotic violence, but also by offering his people hope of a better life with his desire to conquer fertile land and they all were willing to make sacrifices for his dream.

"Wallia looked discontentedly at the road they travelled on; by this time it had become almost impassable with steep corners filled with sharp rocks. The road followed a creek and it was clear that the old Roman trail hadn't been repaired in decades.

"Here it would have been easy for an enemy to ambush, but the scouts didn't report any contact with other tribes, and the slow and arduous here over the pass, deep into enemy territory, had been without incident so far.

"Wallia shook his head over the military stupidity of the Silings who had left such a pass, which would have been easy to defend with just a handful of warriors, unguarded. The scouts had reported that down at the foot of the mountains, where the mountain stream became a river, a small village blocked their way.

"Wallia grinned cruelly: 'There we will test our fighting strength and have some fun,' he shouted to his commanding soldiers, and gave the orders to prepare the attack.

"They charged at the village from the last bend of the road. The staccato of the hooves of their horses as they thundered over the small wooden bridge broke the peace of the quiet village. Women and children washing laundry on the riverbank were the first victims.

"The hardships of the long march across Hispania had irritated the warriors and made them even more aggressive. They now released their lust for violence and murder, using the villagers to exercise their rage.

"Before the men of the village could reach for their weapons, they were already lying in puddles of their own blood with guts hanging out and limbs cut off. Those who were lucky died immediately, while others screamed in pain until their voices reduced to quiet whimpers.

"Wallia saw the bloody activity of his people from his vantage point in the distance and whispered to himself with pleasure: 'Vandals! I will wipe you from this land. Nothing shall be left of you … '

"A thriving, peaceful place had ceased to exist. In the next few days many Silings settlements experienced the same fate. Only then did the leader of the Silings, Prince Fredebal, hastily gather a defensive army and threw it against the overpowering opponent. It became one of the most memorable and difficult battles between the two peoples.

"The Silings, who normally preferred tools and ploughs and now fought with the courage of despair, knew that defeat was close.

"Wallia cursed them and their resilience. He hadn't expected this hard resistance. On the battlefield under the red mountain, which glowed in the sun like burnished copper, the enemies locked themselves in battle. Wallia saw from his vantage point how the ranks of his warriors were beginning to waver. He immediately summoned some of his officers and ordered them to kill anyone who turned to flee.

"When the first fleeing Goths ran into the swords of their own people, panic started to rise in their ranks. But this motivated the Goths to fight with the same hopeless despair as their opponents, and the moaning of the mortally wounded fighters mixed with the sound of the clashing weapons.

"In the end it was a hopeless battle for the Silings. The longer the slaughter lasted, the more the number of able-bodied Vandals who could hold a sword decreased. Soon Prince Fredebal was surrounded only by a few faithful, but they too fell victim to the strikes of the mighty Goths. Only Fredebal remained alive, purely on Wallia's orders. He intended to send him to Rome as spoils of war. With this hostage he wanted to show Emperor Honorius that he, Wallia, would soon be master of Hispania. Fredebal was tied to a tree by his hands and feet and looked at his many slain comrades. The pain in his soul cried out to heaven. He had led his people to destruction, and his conscience would never find rest while his heart was still beating.

"Wallia gathered his troops they visited the Silings villages, which were now exposed to their cruelty without any protection. Any protection they once had was now lying on the blood-soaked battlefield, food for the crows.

"Terrible things happened because the winners knew no mercy.

"Wallia had a penchant for young girls. He had the Vandal girls, who were just maturing into women, brought into his tent and played the strangest games with them. But it always ended the same way – with his guards ripping their clothes off and forcing them to bend over and stretch their naked buttocks towards Wallia. He deflowered these unfortunates one by one, penetrating them with a few strokes and then turning to the next. Wallia was unusually well-endowed and this added to the pain he inflicted on these helpless and frightened girls. He went through the lined-up girls several times before he finally lingered awhile with one and released his semen into her. This signalled the end of his cruel game, and the guards killed the other girls with a short sword blow to the back of their heads. The blood of their young bodies splashed all the way to Wallia and further intensified his excitement which was terrible to behold.

"These were days of cruelty, which did not stop before the native population. But at some point, even Wallia had had enough of his bloodthirsty games.

"Nevertheless, the Goths had paid a high price as well; 15,000 of their finest had met their end by the blade, thus Hispania now felt empty and so parts of it fell under Roman administration again. The surviving Silings and many Alans, who had lost their second King Goa, and now had only one king, Respendal, joined forces with the Hasding Vandals under King Gunderic. All of these united barbarians were now pushed south. As a result of Wallia's actions, the Vandals had lost their significance to us. As a reward, we gave the Goths land. Admittedly, they wanted the most fertile land in Gaul, the Aquitaine. We didn't have much choice back then, so we let them settle there and become *foederati*. Of course, it was clear to us that we had made Gaiseric our enemy. And admittedly he was the one who smashed our empire the most in the following years. I didn't notice it then, but I did know that Prince Gaiseric was very cunning, and he would eventually became even king."

# Chapter VIII

"The unfortunate fact was that, in the Baetica, the Vandals and Alans could not live safely. The Goths, who had settled as *foederati* north of the Pyrenees, could invade Hispania again at any time, and the Suebes were not satisfied with their assigned lands in the north – they could hardly wait to snatch more fertile land from the Vandals. I wish I knew more details about their clashes, but the main thing is that the Vandals and Suebes crossed paths and became enemies again, now the fight was about the most fertile lands of Hispania, And Gaiseric did not need to spend long considering what his options were; right on the other side of the Pillars of Hercules was the famous, fantastic land of Africa. As you said before it was the granary of Rome, with wealth and security at hand.

"But it required the extinction of the Silings, the Vandals had become weaker, and the Suebes sensed a favourable opportunity, the entire Baetica available to take. They attacked the Vandals.

"At that time I was already busy sketching and studying maps of Africa, and it was at this time that a kind of trust, perhaps even friendship, developed between me and Prince Gaiseric. He actually needed any advice he could get, because there was never real peace for them in Hispania.

"After the Goths had decimated the Silings Vandals, Gaiseric realised that they were weakened as tribe. He had pondered for months as to what would be the best for his people, their situation as a tribe wasn't made easier by the fact the Gunderic had become more and more reckless. He had fallen for many sins, especially the wine, and now he was more often a drunk bastard rather than the leader that his people so desperately needed. This was all affecting Gaiseric's mood as well.

"'You seem restless Sire, but yet so thoughtful at the same time,' I finally broached the topic with Gaiseric, after he had kept his distance for the last few months. It even seemed to me that he was keeping his wife and sons at a distance.

"He nodded at me and growled: 'I'm sure it's also become clear to you that we can't stay here in the south of the Baetica any longer. The Goths and their allies, the Suebes, would in time drive us into the sea.'

"I could guess what he was up to and replied he had my full support no matter what he had planned. I took the liberty of making any remarks that I thought would help him, because over the years I had risen from a former slave to his consultant in a way. Nevertheless, it began a period of intense reflection for Gaiseric. Sometimes his doubts overpowered him, but to me he remained strangely open to my advice.

"He asked me, 'Have you ever been on the land on the other side of the sea?'

"'You mean Africa? Never. Are you intrigued by this province?'

"'It doesn't matter what I feel,' he answered slightly irritated. 'We Vandals need a safe place to call home. And Hispania will never be safe for us or the Alans.'

"'You are not thinking of moving your people there, aren't you? Over there, the Romans are strong, it is their most precious province.'

"He stared at me intensely, 'Rome becomes weaker every year. That land over there could well be the perfect place to settle.'

"'Or it could become your people's grave, Sire.'

"He ran both hands through his hair in frustration, 'I am serious about this. But I wonder, could an entire people, with cattle and possessions, be brought across the sea together? The Goths have tried twice and failed miserably.'

"'But your people are no Goths, you have always shown strategy.'"

He nodded and smiled companionly, and then slapped me on the shoulder so hard that I almost fell over.

# CHAPTER IX

The idea to transfer his people from one continent to another was one thing, but to impose it on his own people, raised in the spirit that no-one had the right to tell them what they were supposed to do, was another. The most difficult task was yet to come for him. He had to convince his brother, his people and his tribal princes of the necessity of this project. Meanwhile, his people had settled all over the Baetica. The country and the climate were wonderful. The Vandals got along with the native Iberians and everyone had enough to live. To move them from here would not be easy, and whether the Alans would then follow them was questionable as well. One day, when King Gunderic seemed to be sober, he unexpectedly called an assembly of the tribal princes to Hispalis.

Of course, the Alans and their tribal leaders also took part. It became one of the most memorable gatherings in the long history of the Vandals.

The king rose, but then suddenly let himself fall back onto his throne. He winked at Gaiseric and gestured him forward to address his people.

Like his father, Gaiseric began his speech with a report on the situation of the tribe.

With relentless frankness he described the deadly danger they were in. In melancholy tones he told the crowd what would happen if the Goths, Suebes and Romans attacked them together. After he stopped talking, an awkward silence filled the room. Then everybody was talking they were a mix of confused, wild and excited. It was as though they had woken up from a tranquil dream. When the uproar had settled down, one of the young princes of the Hasding tribe spoke up.

"All the way to Baetica, our enemies have hunted us. We've always fled from them. But now we can no longer escape. Now we must defend ourselves and fight for every foot of this ground. I'm ready, because it is worth it for this prosperous land." The approving applause was thunderous.

"Gaiseric raised his voice again, 'I will now present to you my solution to this situation. I have no intention of escaping either, for I have sworn never to run again. But we will leave this particular place.' Confused murmuring interrupted him. But Gaiseric did not allow himself to be put off and continued, 'We will conquer a new land. A country that is great and rich. We will be masters of a land that has been in the hands of the Romans for centuries. There, too, we will have to fight, and it is not certain whether we will succeed in conquering it. But we will certainly have an abode there forever and the opportunity to build a great and invincible kingdom.'

"Again, everyone seemed confused. 'This is the best land here, so what land are you talking about?'

"Gaiseric raised his hands soothingly to calm his audience, 'I'm talking about Africa. We will create something that no nation has ever achieved before and believe me, I would not consider it if I was not convinced that we can be successful. The truth is we'll never find peace here, even if we survive the next upcoming battle. Then the next one will come, as sure as the sun rises every day. So, my brother and I will go to Africa, and the rest of you can take a month to decide whether you want to follow us or not.'

"'King Gunderic, what you say,' interrupted a chief.

"'Whose Idea you think this is? Do you doubt your king?'

"That was the end of the meeting. The people went into furious discussions. Again and again, the individual chiefs met and argued back and forth, many were against the plan, but most of them stood behind the king.

"The Silings chief always had the loudest voice. 'Gaiseric has saved our people from destruction so many times, even when he was not yet minister of war and first prince. He always knows what he's doing. We should follow him."

"So the meetings continued, and eventually the opponents were brought to silence.

"During this time Gaiseric retired to his part of the palace in Hispalis. In his study he thought through his plans, working out the best way to carry out this great enterprise. He knew there would be trouble. There were so many questions and obstacles before they had even started. How many people had to be transferred to Africa? The people and everything you wanted to take with you had to be counted. How many ships did he need, what kind of ships would be best? How could one organise a crossing so that the tribes could stay together? Would the Alans even come with them? If they did, they would never leave without their horses. How could they be transported safely? Questions after questions piled up in front of him. But now that he had chosen this path, there was no turning back. Step by step, he took on the tasks, solved the problems, planned and thought through everything down to the smallest detail. The days and nights passed so quickly, as if it were only the time of one day."

"Did you encourage him to bring his people to Africa?" Theodoric asked innocently.

"Not really, I just showed him his options, and he eventually believed that it would work. There was only one question left unanswered. Would all of his people and the Alans agree to his plan?"

"'Tomorrow's is our general assembly day, it will bring us the answer,' Gaiseric declared loudly.

"As always happened before a grand meeting of all subtribes began, the meeting was opened with a loud gong. All the princes had taken their places. I was also present, sitting right at the front.

"Gunderic's throne stood on a gallery, so that he could clearly see everyone present. Next to him, Gaiseric sat on a Roman canape.

"'Well, what have you all decided?' Gunderic asked after the gathering had settled down. 'Each tribe shall raise its voice and declare its will with "yes" or "no".'

"'And the will of the majority will be done.' Gaiseric added.

"'We are proud people, we will do it in our own ways,' the Silings chief shouted, followed by a tumultuous roar.

"'Quiet!' Gaiseric's voice thundered through the room. 'I have explained the reasons to you all and it was the truth. Today is not for talking about it anymore. The vote will take place now. The time for talking is over. Now is the time for acting.'

"After this the vote proceeded swiftly, and then it was settled. All of the Vandals stepped forward to their king, as hard as it may have been for some. Finally, the Alans raised their swords one by one, which meant yes. They were surprised by their own unity.

"The brothers looked around the room, satisfied by the result."

# Chapter X

"The elaborate preparations for this gigantic move to conquer Africa were now almost complete.

"Gaiseric had left nothing to chance. All of the necessary work had been planned and carried out down to the last detail. Gaiseric himself had urged the people to hurry up and demanded that every man diligently fulfil his duties or their whole clan would be punished.

"He had the bay of Tarifa converted into a huge port. The former empty beach was now full of long piers constructed on mighty wooden pillars so that even the largest carriages could reach the ships. The census that I helped  to conduct, had shown that 80,000 people had to be transported. They all brought their belongings, wagons and cattle. The census had also revealed that Gaiseric had around 16,000 men fit for battle, of whom approximately 10,000 belonged to the cavalry. This meant that just as many horses had to be transported. That is why most of the fleet had been converted into livestock transporters. Even the Alans nodded contentedly as they inspected the broad vessels that would transport their vast numbers of horses. Initially they didn't believe that so many animals could survive on a ship for several days. Gaiseric was proud of what he had achieved and especially praised the help of the ever-loyal Alans. On his previous voyages he had brought back merchant ships and incorporated them into the fleet, so that they did not have to build many new ships.

"I remember all of those barbarians acting as though they had caught a fever, you could feel an air of change, everyone knew they soon would leave this continent and cross to a new world.

"But one also has to understand these people. One might think that the barbarians, having been awarded land of their own, having finally found peace, would concentrate on cultivating their land and live in peace with the local population, but then they would not have been what they are today. Unreliable barbarians love to make war, everyone against everyone. Even if we Romans did not have our fingers in the pie, the barbarians always found a reason to start conflicts. The Hasding Vandals were dissatisfied with their assigned territory so peace did not last long. There was a conflict between the Vandals and Suebes, led by King Hermeric.

"Anyway, the transition to Africa was planned, and about to be executed.

"Gunderic wanted to be well prepared and had his entire people counted as he had to plan exactly how much ship space the two populations needed for the crossing.

"But Hispania was, and still is, a land without luck. Just as the Vandals were in the last stages of preparations, the plague broke out. It ravaged through the entire peninsula, most affected were the cities and the north. It took a heavy toll, especially on the Suebes. Maybe that was the reason for their astounding reaction.

"Quite unexpectedly, we heard the terrible news. The northern settlements of the Vandals were attacked at night, several families had been massacred in one night. All were slaughtered not even children were spared. As you can imagine, it was the Suebes. They had received wind that the Vandals were on the move and somehow they got it into their head to reduce the number of Vandals and seize the Vandal territory in Hispania before the Vandals left the continent. They thought they could catch the Vandals in a weak moment. Barbarians are always barbarians – they cannot wait, they want everything now and immediately.

"However, this news made King Gunderic furious as I had never seen him before. He immediately called his troops to arms. He wanted to ride north, straight to their capital in Galicia.

"Gaiseric tried to caution him, advising him to convince the Alans to accompany them. But this time his words were to no avail. The next morning, Gunderic hastily gathered his army and the preparations for the voyage to Africa ground to a halt. I somehow gathered that Gaiseric had sent messengers to the Alans without his brothers consent, and they eventually followed the main Vandal army at a distance. However, we were informed that a few Roman units were on their way from the north, not to help the Vandals but the Suebes, as if they had prior knowledge of the upcoming confrontation, which could well be the doom of both peoples. I was already glad that I didn't need to join because the king led this army in person, and made his brother understand that this affair was personal and no place for a foreigner. Besides, me and a few remaining Romans from our old legion were busy manning the ships. The army was already on march when a few warriors returned to our camp with the order to bring me to Gaiseric. We followed the main army along with the Alans, we were actually the reserve in case Gunderic got into trouble with the larger enemy.

"The intervention of a few remaining Roman forces under the new general Asterius Hispaniarum changed the situation when they attacked Gunderic's army on their march north in an ambush. This skirmish wasn't significant, but it forced Gunderic to wait for his brother's troops. We all knew it would come to a pitch battle that would decide the fate of one of the barbarian people.

"Gaiseric was furious with himself. He couldn't catch up and move fast enough with his own army until he finally reached the main part of the army under King Gunderic. On the plateau near the city of Merida, the supposedly most beautiful Roman city of Hispania, the battle between these mighty tribes was beginning to take shape. Gaiseric made an oath on the Bible beforehand that he would not rest until he had wiped out the hated Suebes. Once again it turned out that the emperor probably had his greasy fingers in the game here as well. When the Vandals finally reached the Suebes army, it became obvious that many Suebes warriors wore Roman armour and helmets. The reason for this final confrontation was therefore not only the mutual hatred of the barbarians or land reclamation. Roman gold controls the fate of all barbarians.

"The wide valley with its meadows and fallow fields was well suited for an open battle. Here, so the Vandals thought, they could bring their cavalry with the allied Alans to full advantage.

"There on the opposite field stood the Suebes army with their shields flashing in the sun; the long line up the hill looked like a gigantic flashing line of moving nails moving slowly towards them.

"Gunderic finally listened to his brother Gaiseric, who suggested attacking the Suebes exactly in the centre, while Alan riders attacked them at the flanks.

"The Suebes had mainly foot soldiers, but it was a huge army, outnumbering the Vandals and Alans easily, it seemed they had called all of their people to battle.

"Gaiseric thought the Suebes would probably leave their orderly battle formation and try to fill the gaps that the Vandals had torn in their line. But then the Vandals would attack them from the front and the back, and the Alans from the sides, surrounding and destroying the opponent. Gaiseric saw everything going on in his mind's eye. Then he gave himself a jolt. This was an all-decisive battle, and everything was in his hands. His facial expression changed into that of an attacking lion, an exhilarating feeling seized him. Gunderic raised his sword and pointed forward. Slowly, the attack army set itself in motion. The cavalry stepped forward at the same time, the Vandal center troops set the pace.

"Gaiseric let himself fall back a little to check whether everything was right in his attack formation. In the first row rode the Vandals. Behind them Gaiseric followed his archers and javelin throwers, flanked from both sides Respendial came with his Alans. Satisfied, he saw how his troops showed discipline and followed his idea.

"The Suebes stood with their foot troops four rows deep; their oversized oval, red-coloured shields showing the emblems of the individual tribal princes. In addition, many of them carried long spears to bring the expected on-storming cavalry to a standstill.

"The Vandal units sounded the horns, signaling the attack command. Everyone was now moving slowly towards the Suebes line of defense, then, unexpectedly, Vandal riders rushed forward, and Gaiseric's penetrating tone brought the first line of attack to a halt. They moved wedge-shaped towards the defensive front of the Suebes.

"Orders echoed through the ranks of the Suebes and they transformed themselves from mere foot soldiers into primed weapons, their spears lifted up from the ground and holding them diagonally towards the attackers.

"Thus the Suebes defensive formation solidified into a barrier at which the opponents with their horses were supposed to slit their bellies. The first line of attack of the Vandals had soon reached the defenders. Swinging swords and with a hellish roar, the horsemen raced towards them.

"But when they reached the first Suebes rows, the riders were stopped by this wall of spears, the Vandals tried to strike directly at the Suebes with their long swords but they defended themselves with spears and shields.

"Surprisingly, the Suebes had a small contingent of Franks, placed right in the middle, which the Vandals hadn't noticed before. They were towering fighters who used throwing axes. The Vandal horsemen slammed in the enemy with hesitation but they were either pierced by the spears or became victims of the deadly Frankish throwing axes.

"Gaiseric himself rode forward, screaming, giving orders to avoid the flanks. But they did not advance, the Suebes kept the rows tightly closed, the spears prevented the decisive breakthrough.

"The Vandal horsemen retreated to their starting positions. Gunderic, who observed the events from a hill, gave the order to let the warriors stand in position, as if they were preparing for another attack. Then he had all the Vandal foot troops, admittedly only a few hundred at most, march onto the right wing. For there in the background stood the Suebes king. Gaiseric whished nothing more but to catch him.

"The Vandals gathered then and stormed like an avalanche of spears into the flanks of the Suebes. From a distance you could hear the spears and swords colliding with the shields. Each blow meant splintered wood or severed limbs.

"Gaiseric was still on his horse, it looked dangerous, perhaps his brother would succeed in breaking through, but he rode in full gallop to the far left of the battle field to the Alan king, Respendial, consulted briefly and then the Alan cavalry attacked.

"The Alans swung in towards the flank of the Suebes and at full gallop shot their arrows into their infantry. Of course, they lifted their shields but the arrows were like a black rain from hell, they shot thousands at the Suebes and most found their mark. The Alans kept their distance from the Suebes foot warriors, and so it went on for a time, until it became apparent that the rows of the Suebes were gradually thinning out.

"Finally, to the sound of horns, the small Suebes cavalry sprang into action, the sound of their hooves like a thunder from hell. The Suebes riders screamed and ran forward, trying to reach the Alan riders and throw their spears into their horses. Only a few succeeded, the Alans turned and rode away at lightning speed. Of course, the tight rows of the Suebes had dissolved, they stormed forward like a huge mass of berserkers, trying somehow to catch Alans and Vandals at the same time. That was the moment Gaiseric had been waiting for. He gave the Vandal cavalry the signal to attack again, this time the Vandal horse warriors with their long swords and spears rushed directly into the storming crowd of Suebes soldiers. A bloody massacre began.

"Now there were no more tactics. In the middle the Vandals and Alans pushed into the confused mass of defenders. Spears broke through armour, swords severed limbs and cut open bellies. But the Vandal riders knew their craft well, they struck their targets deep and sideways, and then pulled out their swords to strike a long blow, and whoever they caught usually lost a considerable part of his body.

"It didn't take long until the Suebes, although they still outnumbered the Vandals and Alans, began to lose their stamina. They turned around and some threw away their weapons, stumbled over the bodies and turned to escape.

"Gaiseric gave the Suebes no time to reflect. He had his archers and javelin throwers following the fleeing Suebes and many were killed from behind.

"The shouting on the plain mixed with the neighing of the wounded horses, loud moaning and the crying out for God's help from the dying.

"The Suebes leaders tried to stop the running men, tried to encourage them to push forward again, but nobody listened. Many who stood in their way were trampled down. But this headless escape was of no use to them. The horsemen of the

Alans and Vandals mercilessly pursued the fleeing men and mowed them down one by one.

"Gaiseric blew his horn to gather his warriors. He proudly looked around, it was a terrific victory. His foot soldiers, who had previously formed the attack flank, gradually returned to their original position in small groups. But many shook their heads, they seemed lost, something awful must have happened. Then Gaiseric saw how some warriors were carrying a body on their shoulders. It was his brother, King Gunderic."

"So the great Vandal King Gunderic died in battle?"

"So it was, Theodoric. There were rumours that the Suebes had captured Gunderic alive, tortured him and then killed him. But if that had been the case, then I am sure that Gaiseric had completely wiped out the Suebes.

"So, Gunderic had died in the battle against the Suebes, and then the limping bastard son Gaiseric became king of the Vandals and Alans. Of both you see, because a short time after the battle the Alans lost many of their leaders to the plague. It had mostly affected the natives, but the Alans had mingled with Iberian women and so were immensely reduced

in numbers to the point that they had to subordinate

themselves to the Vandals."

# Chapter XI

"The Vandals had a special way of choosing a new leader. After the battle the Vandal chiefs gathered in one of the restored wagon laagers. All the tents were crowded with people who had experienced much suffering in the past days and listened mournfully to the words of the Arian priest who gave the eulogy and combined it with a divine influence. His words penetrated all of their hearts, the mourning for the king mixed with the mourning for the fallen companions. But he did not reach Gaiseric's heart. He stood there with a stony face at his brother's grave and stared into emptiness.

"The priest finished and made way for Chief Hagard, the oldest Hasding prince who had witnessed the events of the tribe since the times of Pannonia. The old fighter now carried the dead king's shield and sword. He shouted in a rough, tired voice, 'Gaiseric, son of Godigisel, stand before thy people.'

"Gaiseric took two steps forward so that he stood right in front of Hagard who knelt down and laid his shield and sword at Gaiseric's feet. Then he straightened up again. His rough voice continued, 'According to our tradition and the will of the people of the Vandals, you shall be the new king. Whoever objects to this may speak now.'

Hagard turned around and waited. He looked carefully at the princes and Gaiseric. There was a deep, tense silence, but no one spoke. Hagard turned back to Gaiseric, 'If you are ready to lead the people, the tribes of the Hasdings and the Silings and be king of all Vandal tribes, take the shield and the sword of our departed king and carry them for the protection and well-being of the people.'

"Gaiseric grabbed the shield and sword, held them high above his head, and bellowed the war cry of the Vandals. The princes and all who carried a weapon followed his lead.

"Now the Arian priest stepped forward again. His deep, dark voice could be heard right down to the furthest corner of the laager 'You are now the first king of the Vandals to take up royal dignity with the blessing of God, Jesus Christ and the Holy Spirit. May the Lord help you and always show you the right way.'

"Thousands of barbarian warriors cheered and shouted in excitement. Gaiseric raised his hand as a sign that silence should return. The cheering stopped. 'I, Gaiseric, son of Godigisel, hereby promise to bring the people of the Vandals to our promised land to find home as my father would have them reside in. But from now on our path will be different. We will never be attacked again and merely defend, we will attack ourselves.'

The cheering interrupted his speech. Again he raised his hand for silence and continued, 'We will take the time we need and afterwards forget this dark time of mourning for all time, looking to our bright future. I now have one more duty to perform.'

Hagard had listened to Gaiseric's speech carefully and wondered whether he would bow to his father's will, that he should become war minister and head of the army. Now he stepped forward and looked Gaiseric in the eye. He tried to recognise a movement there, but the grey eyes seemed to pierce through him. 'On your knees Hagard,' Gaiseric whispered and took a step back. He raised his sword and laid the flat side on Hagard's shoulder.

"'I hereby appoint you minister of war and advisor to the king. From now on you shall be my right hand, my sword and my shield.'

Everyone was now waiting for Hagard's words. He cleared his throat a little, the emotion of the day had dried his throat but he did not want to croak at this important moment. 'I learned a lot from your father, my dear friend, and I have been waiting for this moment all of my life,' he began, 'You, as well as your father, have shown me your experiences and tricks. I may be old, but I owe my knowledge and ability to your father and I can't replace him. But I will try, with the help of his spirit, to continue the ministry and to serve my people and my king.'

"With those words he stood again. The cheering filled the laager and showed him that the Vandals were in agreement with Gaiseric's decision.

"Now King Respendial stepped forward and approached Gaiseric. He shook hands with the new king. His relationship with Hagard had never been particularly good, he didn't like his fiery, unpredictable nature. The decision to make him Gaiseric's right hand confirmed his fears that relations between Alans and Vandals might deteriorate. 'The Alans will also move south with the new king of the Vandals and his war minister, we will fight with you against the Romans until they no longer harass us and until we have found great lands to settle in, and we will always be at your side when you need us.'

"Gaiseric increased the pressure of his hand. 'The Alans have saved us from great suffering, just as we have saved them in the past. You have thus strengthened our friendship, which should unite us forever," he replied.

"Gaiseric looked around, proud and confident, 'From now on, a new time will begin and I shall be your leader!' he shouted out."

# Chapter XII

"So Gaiseric was now the new king of the Vandals. He immediately set to work organising the departure for Africa. Above the hills of the port city of Tarifa he opened his headquarters, issuing new instructions. Everyone and everything had to leave before the autumn storms set in. The decisive moment of the departure approached daily and the Bay of Tarifa was an indescribable sight. All of the ships of the Vandal fleet were gathered here, this small bay had in a few weeks become the busiest port of the Western Mediterranean. For weeks, horse-drawn carriages had been approaching from all parts of the Vandal's Land. They brought the belongings of the people to the ships, loaded them to their full capacity. All around the bay, up to the wooded heights, Vandals and Alans camped in a tense, expectant mood, eager to set off. Everybody became tired of waiting. The fire from the wandering years had seized them again. The insatiable urge to go forward into the unknown made them restless.

"Personally, I was closer to the barbarians those days than ever before. Of course, I had already become a part of their community sometime before. Yes I am a Roman, I always felt that way, yet the barbarians no longer regarded me as an outsider or even an enemy. I often lived around their families in close vicinity. I helped them where I could, I was far more than a teacher, for many I had become part of their extended family. In the days of preparing to travel, every man was needed. Sometimes I saw Gaiseric nodding his head benevolently to me, I assumed he trusted me, too long have we survived difficult years and often impossible situations side by side. But these days were different, everyone wanted to leave Hispania, from child to old man, they knew only one goal: to reach the African coast safely. No one was afraid of the water, at least not perceptibly. The women were all extremely diligent and worked in a team, encouraging and praising their husbands. They worked, sewed, cut wood and actively showed the children practical things, not like our more feminine Roman women. Not that I detest them, but in

Rome every child is a little god, pampered and fear free. No wonder the Vandals develop into good soldiers.

"On the beach of Tarifa hundreds of open long boats lay side by side, ready to be towed into the choppy waters. A good part of them were captured from the enemy but most of them were self-made. I helped to design the bigger ones which were intended for the Alans and their horses. I helped Gaiseric to count the people, just over 80,000 souls. A few days before our departure, fires burned day and night on the beaches and at dawn after a full moon the first ships slid into the water, these were fully equipped triremes with rudders and sail, reserved for the most experienced warriors. To my surprise, I was to accompany Gaiseric personally on his flagship.

"Gaiseric had invited his closest friends and leaders of the enterprise into the spacious cabin of his command ship for the final briefing. With serious faces they sat at the long meeting table and waited eagerly for their final orders.

"Gaiseric rose. He scrutinised those present. He saw their determined faces, waiting only for his order to leave. 'It is now time, my friends,' he began, 'Today we will leave for Portus Tanger with the first part of our navy. Once we have the city under our control and the moorings are secured, the main transport of our people follow. The rest of the navy will protect the crossings.'

"Gaiseric was silent for a moment, as if he had to consider his next words carefully. 'For our sea crossings, it will be important for the Alans and Vandals to form a unit and act together, especially right after the landing.'

He paused to let his words sink, then his questioning gaze turned on Antony who sat next to me, one of the best sailors of my old legion. 'What does your unerring sense of the weather tell you? Will it last for the next few weeks? We need at least one month to complete the crossing. Our ships need calm seas for they will almost always be overloaded.'

"'There may be occasional storms,' Antony replied dryly, 'but if we don't make the crossing now, we never will.'

"Gaiseric nodded contentedly. That's all he wanted to hear.

"The Arian priest closed his cloak and looked doubtfully into the cloudy sky. 'God will support us, because soon we will bring the true faith back to Africa and free the churches there from the heathens. I've dreamed of this for years.'

"Gaiseric rose. 'Then the time has come,' he announced. 'Everyone knows his job. May God help us all.'

"Horns sounded, with screams and shouts from the crews the ships were pushed from the beach into the sea.

"Gaiseric saw the descent with clarity and composure. He radiated confidence then more than ever. Thanks to his Roman companions he now also understood enough about seafaring to instruct the rear boats using flags and mirrors.

"On that day the water was relatively calm, some of the old warriors even smiled at me. This was the highlight of their lives: a mighty fleet, rough men, weapons, power and a new promised land in sight.

"And we all made it, we arrived on the shore one squadron at a time. Gaiseric's son Huneric with his organisational talent, ensured that the loading of the ships in the bay took place in an orderly manner. We had to be sure that people would not surge onto the boats in a panic, this could lead to the boats sinking or capsizing. Therefore, it was determined who was to enter which boats. Hunerich never tired of reassuring the families that the ships would always come back and that nobody would have to stay behind. Nevertheless, the mood was irritated and often only violence helped to maintain order. But again and again, it became apparent how important it had been that Gaiseric's plans were designed in advance, because except for these small incidents, the loading of the ships was exemplary.

"Nevertheless, it was an indescribable chaos, and it took weeks until the last barbarians with their cargo of people and cattle had passed the strait. Still, the crossing was the greatest logistical event a barbarian tribe had ever accomplished.

"Furthermore, Gaiseric has stormed the Portus Tanger without any loss on both sides.

"The harbour was sheltered in a long bay. Watchtowers at both ends of the coastline guarded the entrance to the port. It used to be the main base of the Roman navy in Africa. Now, however, not a single warship was anchored here.

"The town almost seemed to be abandoned.

"The city had lost its significance. Several times it had been the target of attacks by rebel Berber tribes and had been partially destroyed. The splendour of earlier days was gone. Nevertheless, one could still admire the ingenious master-builder art of Roman architects.

"The Roman garrison seemed to have been deserted for weeks, somehow they knew about the crossings in advance so decided not to take any chances. Gaiseric gathered his people west of Portus Tanger, near rivers and the green fields around the other port on the strait, Roman Port Ceuta. From the beginning, Gaiseric ordered the Vandals to trade and form friendships with the Berbers, the native people of the region. The Vandals had already agreed various agreements with the Berbers before their crossing. Gaiseric knew the Roman troops in North Africa were the main enemy, he did the right thing and allied himself with the Berbers – against Rome.

"After the occupation of the fort, exactly what Gaiseric had expected happened. The common people greeted them as liberators. For too long they had lived under the yoke of the Romans, so anything that came now could only be better.

"Gaiseric had given the order to use force only against the Roman landowners and their guards if they took up arms. However, he gave them a free hand in choosing the means. It took only a few days until the latifundia burned all around the country and supply troops brought food from there to supply the people brought over.

"Of course, the landing at Port Ceuta and Portus Tanger was only the starting point of their journey in Africa. The Vandals had barely landed as the huge trek of people, cattle and wagons started heading west. He intended to bypass the first Roman garrisons, then take the Roman road to Icosium and, finally reaching the wooded and fertile areas around Hippo Regius, the granary and historic treasure chamber of Africa. But there was still a long way to go. However, they planned their journey in stages. The mountains of Numidia were too dry, but 500 miles further west, we knew that the climate became wetter where there was wheat and grass for the cattle. There, in the west behind Numidia, was the first chosen destination. Even before they started the long journey, all of the barbarians seemed to be ecstatic. So far they had all made it alive and well to this new continent, they thought that now it could only get better.

"I must say, I felt genuinely glad for Gaiseric, his friendly smile towards me told me he appreciated my contributions as well. 'It's a wonderful country,' he said. 'Here we will stay, we take the land from the Romans and defend it against every enemy. I tell you the truth, Vitus, any means is fine for me, because there is no going back. Africa is the new home of the Vandals and Alans.'"

"Sire, but this land in Africa is a Roman province, weren't there any Romans around to stop them?"

"The Roman general and provincial ruler in North Africa was Comes Bonifacius, a general of great reputation, however he was involved in constant wars with the native Berbers. Most importantly, he never even believed the Vandals would dare to cross over to Africa. There is still an old rumour that he actually invited the Vandals so they would help him against the Berbers, but I never believed a word of it. Gaiseric is not a king to need an invitation, he took what he had planned. So, when the Vandal fleet actually arrived,

Bonifacius was completely surprised and did everything he could to persuade the barbarians to retreat to Hispania with letters and diplomacy. He was naive and totally underestimated Gaiseric and his determination. A fool."

# Chapter XIII

"Every child and woman knew what was at stake. Here two enormous peoples were on a mission to find fertile land to settle on in a new unfamiliar continent.

"The Vandals and Alans went on long, disrupted expeditions, with their wagons, cattle and families. They headed west along the coastline, until the entire column came to a standstill not far from the city of Calama. News spread like wildfire through the crowds – there was a Roman army near Calama! The famous general and governor of Africa, Comes Bonifacius, had formed a defensive barrier in front of Calama with the help of Gothic auxiliary troops. At the same time his East Roman cavalry could attack at any time.

"Here, not far from Hippo Regius, Gaiseric converted many small villages into fortresses, for he knew that General Bonifacius, though he was involved in wars with Berbers and disgraced at the court of Ravenna by this time, now had to take action against the landed barbarians.

"At first, he didn't have too much to offer. He combed every garrison town for soldiers, bribed the Goths to send him warriors, begged Constantinople for some troops. Actually, both parties sought confrontation, for Gaiseric also wanted to assert himself against some of his rebellious tribal chiefs. These previously unrestricted leaders now saw their power restricted, because by now Gaiseric demanded absolute loyalty and some of the old Germanic traditions had become obsolete to him.

"He was also cautioned by his own princes as well as by his allies. Many chiefs and princes didn't understand Gaiseric's plan as he drove the people further and further west, for many of his fellow countrymen where they had reached was good enough.

"One day, spies came and reported that Bonifacius was marching in the direction of the Vandal and Alan villages and fortifications. Gaiseric summoned me to his tent and I was unexpectedly forced to wear Roman armour. Altogether, we were perhaps several thousand men, the main mass of the

Vandal army lay further to the east, but we marched towards the Romans, and after two days we saw their army.

"Between us and their troops lay a dry valley, behind it flashed the armour of the Roman legionaries, and without a doubt we recognised Gothic cavalry at the wing.

"Who would dare to attack first? I hoped Boniface's troops would just block us, stop our march west. And perhaps that both armies would just withdraw again. We consulted in the evening and drank wine long into the night, and the next morning returned to the positions of the day before. The plan was for the Vandals to attack first. Suddenly, in the middle of the night, the alarm horns sounded. Enemy cavalry was approaching our camp and soon it turned into a merciless slaughter in the darkness of the desert, but our palisades held and the Vandals kept their positions. The next morning there was silence again. So you could call it simply a skirmish, I guess. I looked over the wooden palisades and was startled. There, in front of our position, perhaps only 2 kilometres ahead, Bonifacius' Army was organised in full formation. Their bronze helmets flashed in the sun, to the right of them were Gothic riders, armed with extremely long spears. They stood there almost motionless and waited. They expected us to accept the battle. Gaiseric had the Alans put in line on the right to face the Goths, directly in front of us was the Roman cavalry and behind them the foot soldiers and archers. I thought the Romans were perhaps slightly superior to us in numbers, but Gaiseric probably had the better cavalry. Gaiseric admitted that he had simply not counted on encountering a relatively large army here, which seemed even larger than it had the day before. Perhaps he had underestimated Bonifacius.

Gaiseric patted me on the shoulder, 'You ride towards them, try to speak directly to Bonifacius.'

'"What shall I tell him, king?'

'"You tell him we have a mandate from General Aetius to administer this area. Besides, you're saying that we know that Bonifacius should be recalled to Rome. Tell him that we also know he would be tried for treason there. Understand?' I was so baffled I didn't even know how to answer. And I don't know if he was just bluffing, or if it was actually true. Finally,

I found my voice. 'Who shall I introduce myself as to Bonifacius?'

"'Call yourself Vitus, General of Aetius.'

"'I don't understand my Lord, but I will do it.'

"'Good, because I have learned to trust you, let's go!'

"So I rode forward in full Roman armour and I came perhaps a few hundred meters close to the Roman troops when riders stormed towards me. They surrounded me but said not a word. Then I recognised him, the soldier with the golden crest at his helmet was Bonifacius himself. I said my message to Bonifacius in a loud voice. Surprisingly, he laughed and left the way he had come.

"As soon as I was back in my own ranks, the Alans pushed forward to my right. It was incredible, they galloped towards the Gothic cavalry, then, perhaps fifty meters before they reached the Goths, they swung into a curve and shot their arrows at the Goths from full gallop. The Goths stood there as if carved from stone, many them were pierced by the arrows despite their lamellar armour, but then the infuriated Goths swung into action and pursued the Alans. What I saw then moves me to this day. The Goths followed the Alans with their heavy horses in full gallop, and the Alans slowed down their pace and let the Goths approach them from behind, and just as they had reached a distance of only a few meters, the Alans divided into two groups, some to the left the others turned right. The Goths were irritated, slowing down their speed – a big mistake, because the Alans then appeared on both Gothic flanks and shot their arrows at them from both sides. The Goths screamed and cursed, struck by arrows they fell to the ground like heavy sacks. Some turned and tried to retreat to the Roman ranks, but in vain. The fast Alans caught them so only a handful of Goths made it back to the Roman ranks. But the Alans rode on, far beyond the positions of the Romans who were standing in line. That's where they stopped, waiting for a sign. Horns sounded – Gaiseric's signal to attack. He let his troops march forward in a long row, step by step, more disciplined than I had ever seen Roman legions.

"The Vandals banged on their shields with their swords, and with a terrible war cry they charged at the Roman troops who were still standing motionless in line. It was clearly recognizable, the Romans were now threatened from the front and from the back, caught in a gigantic pincer. Then, in the distance, I saw the sun flashing off the armour as the Romans started to move. But it looked like a movement of chaos and confusion, there was no discipline. And indeed I could see individual soldiers and small groups breaking away from the ranks and running for their lives. Thousands of legionnaires disappeared in a huge cloud of dust and that was it. Gaiseric stopped his troops and the Alans made no more efforts to persecute the Romans. In the aftermath, I must say this skirmish had a greater meaning than I had first thought. Gaiseric could have destroyed the Romans that day, but he chose not to. It was a message to Bonifacius, a warning that he should withdraw, and that he, Gaiseric, was open to negotiation in the future.

But this skirmish was only a slight taste of what was to come. The next day, Gaiseric gave the order to the people of the Vandals and Alans to set off again. We continued further west.

# Chapter XIV

"So the people of the Vandals and Alans moved on. It was the year of Lord 430 when we finally reached the great city of Hippo Regius, the most important trading port of Roman North Africa after Carthage. It was also the city where Bonifacius had retired.

"Gaiseric made it clear to every man that this city was his final destination, when he held it he would dominate the most important and productive area of North Africa. Then, with the capture of this city, they would have gained an almost unassailable position in North Africa, and thus a permanent new home for their people. On the other hand, it was clear that Bonifacius would try to hold it until the last man was slain. For him, it was about holding or going down because the court in Ravenna had forbidden any negotiation with the barbarians.

"We all suspected it would be a long, arduous siege. Of course, we did not know how long and what great privations were to come.

"For 14 months the Vandals besieged the fortified city; it was a cruel siege, followed by an even crueler battle.

"At the beginning, having command of the sea, Boniface was able to keep the city well provisioned. Once again I was an eyewitness, able to closely follow the course of events from a dilapidated castle tower, although the constant dust from the nearby valleys did not make these difficult times any easier for me and the few remaining comrades of the old legion who lived like free men among the barbarians. This city was the first real Roman metropolis on African soil, here General Bonifacius entrenched himself with the remains of his army. The Vandals had the mass of their people dwelling in the eastern city of Icosium. Before Hippo Regius stood over 20,000 Vandal soldiers, plus the Alans and various Berber tribes. Every barbarian looked eagerly at the rich city, which they believed would soon be like a ripe fruit free to plunder.

"At first they tried to storm the city walls. But the walls were too high and too strong. I watched the Vandals slowly but surely build a tower of wood and brick for every mile of wall, connected by trenches. This was to prevent any outbreaks. In the beginning Gaiseric gave the order to build towers on wheels to storm the city walls, but the walls were not only too high, there were also huge ditches and ponds to the wheels could not cross. I must admit that though the Vandals had clever tactics, they didn't understand a lot about sieges. They couldn't end up building towers on wheels, there wasn't enough wood, and the Romans had catapults and *ballistae* for which the Vandals had no defense. Every time we approached the walls, the Romans shot gigantic arrows at the Vandals, who suffered great losses and did not dare to get closer to the walls. From the towers above, Roman soldiers called out as loudly as they could to insult the barbarians, but some paid a price for their insolence – the barbarians have a keen eye and once they had taken the city they recognised most of these brazen soldiers. They let the caught soldiers live, but only after they had cut out their tongues, some were also castrated with blunt knives. During the siege the barbarians cut off the fresh water aqueducts, the port was totally sealed off from the fleet and, although the city was big, there were difficulties at first to seal off the city completely.

The barbarian saying was true that only rats managed to leave a besieged city. But, on the other hand, many people were let in, every man was needed to reinforce the weakened troops. As weeks turned into months, the rotten smell of excrement and smoke could be perceived even further behind the walls.

"Many members of the population, including farmers, craftsmen, the simple folks and slaves but also the resident Berbers, stood openly or secretly on the side of the barbarians. Many tried to flee from the trap, we received almost daily reports about the conditions of the city, where they were running out of resources.

"Three months into the siege, the famous Catholic bishop Augustine, who was already 77 years-old, died. Many said it was because of the famine, or perhaps of stress and sorrow, because he was not an Arian Christian like the Vandals but a Roman Catholic, which the barbarians hated.

"There was a devastating famine in the city, as the wheat fields outside the city lay dormant and unharvested. The Vandal fleet also blocked the entrance to the waterway.

"This combined with the death of the bishop was a shock for the senate of the city as well as for Bonifacius, the people considered it an ill omen and the senate gathered for an emergency meeting.

"Bonifacius had called together his officers, senators and representatives of the church in the auditorium of the palace for a discussion of the situation. Everyone had to submit a report for their area.

"The first speaker was Porcius, the Bishop of Calama, who had just escaped from the city with his life, 'The punishment of the Lord has come upon us. The Antichrist Gaiseric rages in the cities and villages. He persecutes and torments our steadfast servants of God, who at the behest of our former chief shepherd, Augustine, are not allowed to leave their place until the last parishioner is safe.'

'Bonifacius interrupted, 'Are you saying that we Romans are also sinners? Watch your tongue, Bishop!'

"Porcius continued shyly, 'Forgive me, General, but I speak only of the barbarians, the Vandals. These heretical barbarians have their eye on our sisters in the monasteries. They constantly endure the carnal lust of these savages.'

"Bonifacius shook his head angrily. "I did not witness any of that myself, nor have I heard of any mass rapes by the Vandals. As bishop you are also a Roman chronologer, let me tell you, the barbarians are not innocent, but there is no reason to exaggerate and further inflame the situation!'

"The bishop folded his hands and continued, 'The word of God has fallen silent in this land. Instead, the Arian heretics are now preaching from our robbed and desecrated churches and forcing people to pay homage to this heresy. Truly, I tell you, the apocalypse is near.'

"The silence that followed his speech was interrupted by Bonifacius clearing his throat, he now wanted to give his report on the military situation. He wasn't comfortable either, he knew that the bishop was prone to embellishment, and his reports would probably be repeated by other Roman historians.

"Bonifacius' report on the military situation was similarly devastating. In short, concise sentences, he described the unsuccessful attempts with individual failures of his reinforcements from Italy to open new supply routes. He spoke of the dwindling morale of the legionnaires and criticised the lack of care for his soldiers from the nobility while the wealthier officials lived as if nothing had changed and there weren't barbarians outside the city.

"'But our Roman soldiers remain undefeated,' said Bonifacius, 'And the two most important cities have withstood the attack of the barbarians. These were the large metropolis Carthage and just here Hippo Regius. The enemy will certainly not succeed in one thing, he will never set foot in this city!" He thundered this last statement and looked around, expecting the chamber to ring with applause. But no hand moved.

"The speaker of the senate, Gaius Volusianus, rose and began his own report, 'The speeches of my predecessors have brought us nowhere. Action must be taken. The city won't be able to endure this siege for much longer. At the head of our holy church we apparently have a pastor who is not interested in the situation of our country, who gives nonsensical instructions to his servants of God and thus places them in the hands of their tormentors. In the Comes Bonifacius we seem to have a military leader who has made so many mistakes while defending this province that I don't have enough fingers on my hands to list them all.'

"Bonifacius interrupted furiously, 'Watch your tongue, Volusianus, otherwise I might have those fingers cut off for you. Then you'll never lead this senate again!'

"Volusianus refused to be impressed by his words and continued in a cold voice, 'I know you don't want to hear the truth. The fact remains that the city will not be able to endure the siege for much longer. When will the promised help finally arrive? When will the emperor send a fleet to help us? If reinforcements don't arrive soon and chase the barbarians out of this country then we are lost.'

"Bonifacius replied undaunted, 'According to the latest reports, the Byzantine fleet has already sailed. General Ardabur Aspar, the most powerful man in the Eastern Roman Empire, is to command them himself. With him we will restore order throughout the country.'

"Volusianus replied sceptically, 'Pray for this to happen soon, Bonifacius, otherwise the senate will have to begin expelling refugees from the city.'"

All this has been handed down to me.

The barbarians did not manage to penetrate the city, but Gaiseric was of the opinion that he would succeed only at great losses that he could not afford. Spies reported time and again that Constantinople was about to send ships and troops, but nobody knew when they would come- if they came. Gaiseric came to the conclusion that with every day, time was playing against him and he could not control it. This was exactly the kind of situation that he hated, and he became more and more agitated and unpredictable as time went on.

Every day he rode along the city walls. Gaiseric stared at the mighty walls and towers of Hippo Regius with hatred. They seemed threatening and invincible as they stretched themselves into the sky and blew the standard of the Legion of the Comes Bonifacius from the towers.

# Chapter XV

Gaiseric clenched his fists and cursed at the enemy. You could see him walking through the camp for weeks, his face tight with agitation. He told me that there were only a few independent bastions left in the country. This was once the fortress of Cirta, enthroned high up on a mountain ridge, where it was as good as impregnable. It did not interest him because it dominated the entrance to the anti-Arian Donatist sects and the Moorish mountains far to the south. However, Gaiseric did not intend to sacrifice even one man to storm these cities of different people; he would rather let the Western Empire become fragmented.

Now only Hippo Regius and Carthage remained, but after fourteen months, Gaiseric was short on supplies. Day and night he pondered his options.

The thought of Carthage alone made him uncomfortable. This huge metropolis of Africa with one million souls could easily pit two hundred thousand soldiers against him, and he racked his brain as to why they didn't do it. Because of this

Gaiseric had not dared to attack Carthage except for a few skirmishes surrounding the city.

But without this city, which was equal in splendour and importance to Rome, his victory in this land would not be complete. Everybody knew that the fall of Carthage would be the death blow to the Western Roman Empire, yet Hippo Regio was the only hindrance that stood between Carthage and the Vandals, and Hippo Regio still held out.

The news did not get any better. It was already spring and I happened to be in Gaiseric's tent when a scout stormed in.

"Bad news, Sire! Our observers on the coast report that a large fleet of at least two hundred war galleys has entered the Bay of Carthage."

Gaiseric did not show any emotion, but his thoughts were churning. Only the Eastern Romans in Byzantium were able to bring this many warships against him. In contrast to the Western Empire, the Eastern Romans had not neglected their fleet, which secured the coasts of the Aegean Sea and certainly counted over a thousand ships. The fact that they only arrived with two hundred ships showed Gaiseric how surely they felt they could defeat him. This may have been his chance. Never before had the situation here in Africa been as threatening as it was now, as the emperor in Constantinople interfered directly.

He immediately held a council of war, which I was also allowed to listen to:

"We can't let them out of Carthage," he said. Respendial nodded.

"We should beat them first; then the city has no hope of anything."

The Vandal king stepped towards his friend and stretched his hand out.

"I truly believe this will be our last campaign. The Western Empire is all but finished."

"Don't forget us when Carthage will be divided like a piece of sweet bread." Respendial's's face flashed in hidden excitement.

"And Rome will be mine," Gaiseric whispered.

Now the course was clear; the army would be assembled as Vandals and Alans gathered for their final battle.

Gaiseric's orders came sharply and without hesitation.

"Two thousand cavalry and three thousand foot soldiers remain here before Hippo Regius. Let no man nor mouse in or out. The Vandal fleet remains here in position outside the port. I don't want any contact with the Byzantine fleet at sea; at this moment we can't have the loss of even a single ship. The rest of my force will go with me to Carthage. There the fate of our people will be decided."

The Vandals lifted the siege, though this granted the Romans a slight victory. However, as soon as the siege was lifted Bonifacius fled the city by sea undetected, as he was eager to meet with reinforcements from Constantinople. Then the Vandals were able to finally occupy Hippo Regius without any more sacrifices. However the subsequent battle is the one that we will remember in generations to come.

At the time, I didn't understand why Bonifacius waged an open battle after giving up the city. Today, however, I believe that if he hadn't done it, he would have lost his head in Rome. At that time all kinds of rumours circulated in Rome that Bonifacius had brought the Vandals into the country to defeat the Berbers, and that he even had a secret understanding with Gaiseric. The rumors went that he had done so not only to save his reputation, but because he wanted to be king of North Africa. Rome has always been a rumor mill, but I am sure that the *Magister Militum*, General Aetius, had his dirty fingers at the heart of it.

Regardless, Bonifacius decided to fight. He had received substantial reinforcements from Constantinople that included even barbarian auxiliaries and were led by Flavius Ardabur Aspar, a barbarian general, *Magister Militum* of Theodosius II and an Alan himself. I remember I was already afraid for my own head, having been a guest of the Vandals for such a long time, which by Roman standards could be interpreted as a sign of treason. Here before Hippo, a well-equipped and numerically superior army stood against the united peoples of the barbarians. Perhaps for the first time in decades there was a chance to show the barbarians that Rome could never be defeated.

Theodoric shook his head in disbelief. "So, whose side were you on at that time?"

Vitus took a deep breath and shouted out as loud as he could. "How dare you ask me such a question, young man?" But from the look at Theodoric's innocent face he knew he meant it. And why not tell the truth, Vitus thought, as he scratched his chin and sighed. "I secretly hoped that Rome would remain the ruler of the world, but, Gaiseric was my friend and a man of reason. The Vandals had a right to migrate, and Rome had disgraced itself and needed to change." He paused, and when there was silence he went back to his story. "The battle itself began rather slowly. The two armies looked at each other for most of the day, standing idly opposite each other at the appropriate distance."

# Chapter XVI

Hippo's walls stood far in the distance while the ranks of the two Roman armies advanced toward each other over the dusty field between the barbarian host and the city they deSired. I watched from the top of a hill, among wagons and tents of the Vandal army, silently in awe of the glory of Rome.

Bonifacius, count of Africa, who had skillfully frustrated King Gaiseric's attempts at taking Hippo for over a year, was marching out of the city at the head of two reinforcing armies One was from the Western empire and one from the Eastern. Splendid banners and golden eagles stood high among ranks of spearmen as the army advanced safely behind an interconnected shield wall. Even from this far away I could easily imagine the *palatini*, the best of the best, surrounding the golden eagle, an ancient symbol of martial excellence, the treasure of the army, and the pride of those who protected it.

Around them, regiments of *comitatenses*, hardened professional soldiers, formed a line more than eight ranks deep, protecting the archers. In turn, they were protected by a screen of lightly armed skirmishers. *Spatha* and *contus*, respectively the sword and the heavy spear of the Roman infantry, were an extension of the body to any true warrior of the old empire. Watching that spectacle, I could almost feel the sword dangling at my side and the spear in my hand. I would have given anything to be among those marching down there in the dust on this glorious day.

Green, beautiful farmlands could be seen in the distance from the hill. It was a clear, sunny day and my sight could reach far. The so called "breadbasket" of the Roman empire could be seen in all its beauty north of the battlefield, near the city and along the coast. The lush, vivid green was marred by blackened and burned areas, the product of the Vandal's raids. The battlefield itself was far less green. Dry land, separated from the coast by low hills and unforgiving winds, formed the perfect arena for the two armies. Dust and sand pushed by the wind from the southern desert covered this unforgiving plain like a carpet.

I gazed at the Roman line as it advanced slowly and carefully, with large contingents of cavalry protecting its sides. For a beautiful instant, I could feel the certainty of victory. How many were among the lucky blessed who were fighting for the empire? Thousands, maybe tens of thousands; certainly enough to match the Vandals and then some. Finally, the Vandals and Alans were about to fight the greatest military in the world at its best. This time, Rome would finally triumph.

These thoughts lasted just a moment. My long captivity had changed my point of view too much. What I experienced in Spain and during the first confrontation between Bonifacius and King Gaiseric couldn't be ignored, even in front of this magnificent spectacle. How many of those *palatini* and *comitatenses*, after thirty years of almost uninterrupted civil war, were really worthy of their position? Most were lower grade soldiers from barbarian tribes, elevated to such a rank for lack of better options. How many of those men could perform at the level expected of them? I took a second look at the Roman force and I saw that it was split into two different armies, led by different people, and used to different opponents and tactics. Even from this far I could recognize the Eastern empire troops, standing out from the Western soldiers with the bright colors of their clothes and their standards.

Many in the Roman army were assuredly Arians, of the same Christian doctrine as the Vandals. Bonifacius was baptized by an Arian and Aspar was one, just like many among the locals in Africa. To some of them the Vandals could even look like holy warriors, fighting for the true faith. The more time passed, the more the Imperial army looked scraped together from what was left of a bloody war, divided into two different forces and formed by men from faraway lands. They had little to gain from victory and were led by a man who had already retreated in front of the Vandals to seek refuge between the walls of Hippo.

I moved my attention back to the Vandal army, a far more disorganized force, made out of a smaller infantry contingent and a huge amount of both light and heavy cavalry. But I knew Gaiseric had already proved himself to be a resourceful and aggressive leader. I also knew he was far more cunning and shrewd than any of his contemporaries

The Vandals had changed during the years spent in Africa. Already great riders, they found they could learn much from the hit and run tactics of the Berber and Moorish tribes. These were the same riders who fought centuries ago in Hannibal's army and the same Moorish who encircled and massacred the Romans at Cannae.

I felt tense. Nervous. I looked at Gaiseric's army, made of two different confederations of tribes, and saw one. One force, following one Arian faith and one King, fighting to carve their own kingdom out of the empire.

Large wagons, used to transport everything the Vandals owned, formed a circle behind Gaiseric's lines, a makeshift fortress to be used in case of emergency.

Drums started pounding from the Roman formation, as the battle line had almost reached a suitable distance for the archers to begin their work. I had to be closer to the fight to see, so I began to walk toward a better vantage point. My keeper followed me but didn't seem to mind the unexpected walk, as he wanted a better viewing spot himself.

Hours passed. Hours of skirmishing and brief, explosive moments of contact. Every time the two infantry blocks made contact, the Roman tactical superiority became apparent even from a distance. The first line of shields focused on forming a defense to keep the enemy at bay, while the second line was entrusted with the offense. The Vandals were far more capable as one on one fighters, and while they had learned a lot during the past few decades, they still looked like an unruly mob in front of the Imperial army.

Roman spears were heavy and capable of penetrating most defenses. Arms were pinned to their shields by broken spearheads. Lucky blows would pierce the front of a Vandal's helmet from time to time in gory scenes I don't dare recall. Slowly, the Romans made their enemy pay the toll of prolonged battle. The Roman center advanced in perfect order under the watch of Aurelius Anicius Symmachus, my friend and veteran who held the whole of Africa years before. Even in his old age he still towered over the center of his formation, motionless like a statue, unyielding as a true Roman should

be. Leadership certainly played a role in this battle, as the

Vandal infantry was led by King Gaiseric's son Huneric, who

was still young and inexperienced.

I stopped almost at the end of the hill's slope. The battle

was still quite far, but lower in the plain the heat of battle was

stronger. The Alans and the Vandals kept moving, throwing

themselves at the Roman front to deliver their deadly

projectiles and then scattering back to the main formation. On

both sides the forces were constantly maneuvering, each

trying to outflank their opponent. Watching the Roman

infantry keep up the slow advance, I was again filled with

hope for the Romans. Bonifacius' plan was clearly to frustrate

the Vandals, to minimize losses and to goad them into a

raging frontal assault. If they could resist the initial fury of the

barbarians and tire them out, the superior efficiency of the

Roman infantry would win as it had so many times before. It

was a sound plan, perfect against the previous Vandal King

but far too simple for a man such as Gaiseric. From my

vantage point I watched in awe as the King's counter-ploy took form in front of my eyes.

Huneric, first son and heir to the Vandal King, moved along the battlefield behind the screen of dust that filled the area between the two armies. The prince carried a yellow flag at the tip of his spear, screaming orders and gathering troops from various sectors of the battlefield. I only understood the meaning of this after he managed to gather a solid wall of the heavy Alan cavalry, armed with spears, into one block of troops on the right flank.

While the Vandals formed the backbone of the army, the Alans were people of the steppes, meaning they were adept at two tactical approaches: horse archery and devastating charges. The Alan heavy cavalry, their most renowned warriors, could be distinguished by their pointed helms and shining scale armor. Prince Huneric, young and still anxious to prove himself, rose his flag and signaled the charge. The drumming of thousands of horses galloping across the field reached me like a slap in the face. An impenetrable dust cloud rose to cover both the Alans and the Roman cavalry's counter charge, a line of cataphracts from the east.

Under the dusty cloud no one could know who was prevailing. From my position I only saw the climactic first impact. The horses, from both sides, moved to fill any free space in the enemy formation, trying desperately to avoid frontal impacts while spears and swords clashed against shields. A cacophony of screams and ringing impacts rose, louder even than the hoofbeats had a second before. After a few minutes dust was everywhere, settling in dense clouds, and all that remained was the sound of battle.

It was then that Gaiseric's plan became surprisingly obvious to me. It didn't matter who would have won the encounter. Looking at the Roman force Gaiseric had seen two separate armies, just like I did; he was going to gamble that one would not risk sacrificing itself for the sake of the other. This also meant, of course, weakening the Romans' left flank with a charge led by Theodoric, Gaiseric's younger son. If Gaiseric's plan didn't work, he would find himself in a losing struggle against his Roman counterparts.

Aspar and his eastern forces, instead of following Bonifacius' plan, started giving ground, afraid of having Prince Huneric and his riders on their flank. Bonifacius had taken command of both armies, but Aspar was a general in his own right and chose to turn away from the new threat. As I looked at the center of the Roman army, I couldn't identify Aurelius Anicius Symmachus anymore. The infantry commander must have been riding along the line, screaming to hold, but to no avail. Just like in the skirmish at Tarraco, the Roman formation bent and then broke. Large holes opened between the differing units, quickly filled by the charging Vandal light cavalry. What was supposed to be, in the mind of Count Bonifacius, a precise tactical battle was turned into a chaotic all-out melee, where the barbarians could not be bested.

Gaiseric, surrounded by his personal guard, rode up to the front of the line, splitting it in two and turning himself into the tip of a terrifying spear made out of his whole army. Theodoric and his infantry followed their King, their war drums joining the chaos reaching my ears. Their charge joined the skirmishers, now furiously contesting the open spaces among the Roman infantry, and pushed through. The King and his son met in the heart of the Imperial force.

The valley where I had seen hope and glory, where I watched Rome show all of its magnificence was slowly covered in red. I saw lone Roman soldiers trying desperately to fight off the overwhelming Vandals. The archers were mowed down in a frenzy by the victorious enemies. The battle was over, and now came the slow slaughter of those not lucky or fast enough to flee back to Hippo.

Finally Hippo Regius fell and the last Roman soldiers were shipped back to Rome and Constantinople as Gaiseric made it the capital of his new North African empire. The barbarians had captured enough soldiers, and they would give a good ransom and perhaps even negotiating power. Gaiseric had his plans and I could almost guess them.

# Chapter XVII

Vitus put both hands behind his head and closed his eyes.

"This, young man, was also the time when Gaiseric finally offered me the chance to return to Italy not only as a free man but also his ambassador. For me, the question was whether I should stay with Gaiseric or go back to Rome where I was probably long forgotten? What do you think, young man?"

Theodoric's face gleamed with delight.

"You stayed with the king! Why did you not leave?"

Vitus smiled and refilled his goblet.

"You must know, this king was a very generous and honest fellow, a proud warrior who who never lied to me. Loyalty was paid back with the same." Vitus looked up to the dark ceiling, and his eyes seemed to be flickering with memories of the past.

Theodoric swallowed and tried to focus. "So after the king won, what were his plans, Sire?"

Vitus sensed they needed a break.

"Young man, we'll talk again in a moment, as my long awaited visit approaches. The famous General Macian, an old friend of mine, has finally arrived in Rome."

Vitus clapped his hands and the mighty doors opened. Flanked by two guards, a tall middle-aged man, whose face was long and scarred, approached. From his looks he appeared to hail from some Syrian or eastern province, and his posture along with his bronze breastplate revealed a battle hardened officer who had acquired great dignity.

Marcian and Vitus embraced each other, and the two laughed heartily as Vitus opened another amphora of wine.

"Theodoric, get up, bow before my friend. He will also have interesting things to tell you about King Gaiseric."

Theodoric immediately got up and bowed in awe.

"Well then, young prince," Marcian said. "You have before you the best teacher of the Roman Empire, especially considering that Rome is endangered by the very man you are being taught about." General Marcian grabbed a goblet. "Go on, young man, ask what you must. Time is of the essence."

Theodoric looked up, confused.

"Sire, what is your experience with this king? Do you know him too?"

With a wave of his hand Vitus interrupted.

"Just a moment, Marcian. Listen, Theodoric, my day of liberation came when I first met my present friend Marcian, and for me it was the first day of a new life. For Marcian it was also something like a new beginning. It began after the Battle of Hippo Regius. Marcian was an officer under Aspar and took part in the battle of Hippo. Marcian, why don't you tell the young man yourself how it happened?"

Marcian chuckled.

"Yes, I took part in the battle. I am sure Vitus has already told you about the legendary battle at Hippus Regius. These were also the days when I met this Gaiseric."

"You met him in battle?"

"No, young prince, or else either I or Gaiseric wouldn't be alive. But I admit, for a short time I was actually his prisoner." The General cleared his throat. "If I were there today I would never think that I'd get out of there with my life. But I was unconcerned at the time as only youth can be.

After I was captured in the battle of Hippo by the Vandals,
I remember sitting in front of a well. My fellow prisoners
were desperate; they feared torture, but somehow I was
unburdened. I played with a stick and watched the king where
he was standing on a veranda, looking over us. Gaiseric
watched from the shaded arcades of his porch out onto the
Roman prisoners. His war minister snuck up behind his
master, and it seemed as if a strange restlessness had driven
him out. He had important news for his king. Gaiseric felt the
tension.

"What news have you brought me?"

The general pointed to the court and then pointed to an
eagle flying high in the air. Gaiseric didn't understand at first,
and he waited for something to happen. But nothing did.
Again he let his gaze wander over the prisoners, saw how they
were crowded together in the few shady places and looked up
at him full of hate. Then his eyes fell on a young Roman who
did not take heed of the sun. He lay stretched out in the
middle of the courtyard, unprotected in the blazing sun, and

slept. His torn and dusty uniform indicated that he was one of their leaders.

Gaiseric shook his head over such arrogance and began to look away when something strange happened. First he heard the beating of wings and then the cawing cry of the eagle above. The mighty bird of prey, symbol of Roman power, and adornment of every standard of Roman legions, circled the court with its wide wings. Gaiseric looked up at him with interest. He had never seen this shy bird of prey so close before.

The beast's circles became tighter and tighter until he stopped in one place in the middle of the courtyard, flapping his wings violently. At first Gaiseric assumed that the bird had spotted prey there and would attack it at any moment. But nothing of the sort happened. The eagle only stopped in the air and spread his mighty wings.

Gaiseric's gaze was then drawn to something that almost took his breath away. The wings of the eagle gave the young Roman down there in the courtyard shade so that his head was no longer exposed to the blazing sun. Gaiseric closed his eyes.

Suddenly he knew where he had seen all this before; in his dreams, the omen he had been waiting for since he arrived in Africa. He opened his eyes wide. The eagle above the yard was no longer there. The young Roman woke up and stood.

Gaiseric called for his bodyguard.

"Bring this man down there to me at once. I have to talk to him," he ordered excitedly.

The bodyguard wondered about his king, but carried out the order without asking.

A short time later, this young Roman who I hardly remember being now stood before Gaiseric. I was forced to kneel in front of him, and he looked me over from top to bottom. He must have seen a young man who resembled the statues that were on every corner of this Latifundie. Short, black, curly hair framed a flat, bare face. He looked at me with intense interest.

Finally he said in a low voice, "It is not every day that a Roman prisoner such as you stands before me. There's something special about you that I need to figure out. What is your name?"

I remember I hesitated to speak and to reveal any information so I just shook my head.

Gaiseric smiled.

'As you can imagine, we have ways and means to make you speak. Please don't make me use them. Let's just have a little chat, and nothing will happen to you.'

I laughed contemptuously.

"No physical pain could cause me to speak against my will." Gaiseric nodded seriously.

"I understand," he replied gently. "But look down into the courtyard, where your fellow soldiers are crowded under the shade. For any unanswered question, we'll cut off one of their limbs and stuff it in their mouth. How about that?"

I stared at him with a penetrating gaze, but then I gave in and said, "I know you do exactly as you say, Barbarian King. I don't want unnecessary bloodshed. I am Marcian, the servant of General Aspar." Gaiseric stood.

"You are Aspar's right hand and favourite of Emperor Theodosius?" By the time I nodded in response, Gaiseric was already in control of himself again. He could hardly believe it, but the luck of the battle had played a person of immense importance into his hands. He immediately made a plan. First of all, he cleverly hid his joy at my catch and asked, "Why does Aspar send such an outstanding person as you into the front lines?"

"I should have only commanded the cavalry attack, but when the first riders fell, I moved to attack the flanks. I advanced too far and my horse was hit by an arrow."

"I saw that and I let your cavalry go nowhere. That's why you stand before me now." He smirked, and I had to agree.

"Like a beginner I walked into your trap and therefore I deserve to be your prisoner. Kill me or send me into slavery. It would be a just punishment."

Gaiseric laughed.

"Your miserable appearance insults my eyes, Marcian, servant of the almighty Aspar. I'll give you a chance to freshen up a little. This property has an excellent thermal spa, which will satisfy your high-born tastes. My servants will give you new clothes, Roman clothes. Then we'll meet again and continue our little conversation."

Theodoric shook his head in disbelief. "He did not harm you at all?"

Marcian smiled in memory while Vitus leaned against the wall with a grin. Vitus cleared his throat.

"And then I was called," said Vitus. "I excitedly explained to Gaiseric the importance of his capture. "Marcian is in our hands? Do you know that in Byzantium he is spoken of as the future emperor? You'll be able to demand a grand ransom for his release."

Gaiseric shook his head. "I'll let him go like this and you'll see it earns me more than all the gold they'd offer me."

I looked at him in confusion, as didn't understand his intention. "What are you going to do with him?"

"You'll see," Gaiseric replied, and his voice resonated with something like triumph.

But I will finish this little episode. In the late afternoon Gaiseric and Marcian met again. Forgive me to say, Marican, but you as a young Roman were almost unrecognizable. Freshly washed and dressed in a white tunic, you looked like a young god. The bath in the spa and the new, clean clothes had given him dignity and personality back. Gaiseric noticed the change and was delighted about it. Somehow he must make it so that Marcian did not see in him and the Vandals such a despicable enemy.

Gaiseric asked Marcian to sit. Since it was a Roman custom, they sat on the floor. Servants brought pillows on which they could make themselves comfortable, and thereupon food was brought for such a spoiled Roman tongue to enjoy.

"But I was still suspicious of him, and I scrutinized my host." Marcian added. "Since the time of my capture, I had laid in the dust and eaten nothing, but I was not so easily swayed.

"Now that you know my name, you treat me like a dear guest. Do you think I'd betray Aspar for a chop of lamb?"

Gaiseric laughed and laid a hand on my shoulder. Then his face became serious again, and his grey eyes seemed to penetrate me to my skull.

"I would never ask such a thing of you, for I despise traitors." Gaiseric laid back in his pillows. "I want to tell you something about me and my people, and I don't want you to be disturbed by the growling of your stomach. So take this offering and forget for a moment that you are my prisoner."

I remember my hunger was overwhelming, so I put my concerns aside and gave in. I ate until I was full, and the servants made sure that my wine cup was never empty.

"I also need to mention something significant," Vitus interrupted. "They had a brilliant conversation. Gaiseric slowly managed to dispel Marcian's distrust. He told him the story of the march of the Vandals and Alans through the old lands in Germanica and Hispania in search of a new land. Of course, Gaiseric only reported what young Marcian was supposed to hear. But this was enough to change Marcian's opinion about Gaiseric."

Marcian nodded. "And now I must honestly say, slowly I began to secretly admire this king, who caused such difficulties for the Western Roman Empire, even though he remains our enemy to today.

Eventually I asked him, "Great king, what are you going to do with me now?" But he pretended not to understand my question. In my naivete, I kept pushing, and asked an even more impolite question. "How many gold coins would you charge for my release?"

Gaiseric was silent for a while. Then he took a deep breath and answered.

"I have declared war on the Roman Empire only because we have been given no choice. Our people need space in which they can live in freedom. Rome has always denied us this; that's why I'm taking it now. My hatred for you Romans has not diminished, but I like you and we could be good friends if we weren't on different sides. That's why I'm letting you go. You can take your men with you."

I was amazed beyond all expectations.

"Just like that?" I asked. "No ransom? No strings attached?"

Gaiseric feigned embarrassment. "Not quite. I don't want to face you on the battlefield again. Therefore you must promise me that you will never again raise arms against me and my people. My other request is that I'd like to speak to General Aspar. Take this message to him and make sure that a meeting takes place. Give me your word that you will abide by these conditions, and then you will be free."

I pondered for quite a while and looked at Gaiseric piercingly. I feverishly searched for a trap or a catch, but I could not find one.

"You will truly let me go on these terms?"

Gaiseric nodded silently and reached out his hand to me.

"Give me your word and you'll be my guest from now on. You can go with your people whenever you want." We shook hands like equals.

"You have my word," I said, not knowing that I had thus sealed the continuation of the Vandal kingdom in North Africa.

"And the king just let you go," Theodoric asked, astonished.

"It is true." Marcian patted Vitus on the shoulder.

"That was also the time when the last of the lost legionaries from Gaul were finally released into freedom," Vitus added. "I was not released officially until after the sacking of Carthage, though I was with them of my own will.

I admire Gaiseric's foresight at the time. Marcian and the mighty general of the East, Aspar, have not since undertaken a campaign against the Vandals. No one knows exactly what Gaiseric and Aspar discussed, but they had reached an agreement, a non-aggression pact.

"Soon it will be light, Vitus," Marcian said. "Now we have the chance either to go to sleep or to tell this young man the rest of the story." He pointed to the young prince, whose eyes shone just as brightly as they did a few hours ago.

"As long as the wine is flowing, we will continue to tell the old stories and teach this young man lessons," Vitus said. "The fact is, Hippo Regio has belonged to the Vandals ever since. Gaiseric was a good ruler, as shortly after conquest of Hippo the city came again into full bloom. Business flourished, thanks not only to the extensive pirate journeys of the barbarians, but also because the population was liberated from the Roman tax collectors and could do whatever they wanted - at least as long as they did not stand in the way of the barbarians.

Gaiseric even reopened the university and teaching rooms of the Senate. And in his great modesty, he even let me lead this institution. But I knew Gaiseric wanted more; he wanted to be the most powerful man in the Mediterranean, and he needed living space for his people. To achieve this he would use any means whatsoever.

His son Huneric had married a daughter of the Visigoth king, but the highest gains could be achieved in Rome itself. There he needed a high prince who had influence and was married into the Imperial family. Huneric wasn't quite happy with his prudish wife, and Gaiseric had never forgotten the attack by the Visigoths on the Silling Vandals in Hispania. So the Vandals cut off the good woman's nose and ears and sent her back to her father, the Visigoth king.

Huneric quickly became husband of Eudoxia, daughter of Emperor Valentinian III. See, Gaiseric was a man who had talent to recognize opportunities, form new alliances and sow hatred among his enemies. Through the marriage, the Vandals became temporary allies of Rome, united against the dangerous Visigoths who threatened his position in the western Mediterranean. Nevertheless, Gaiseric was not yet finished. He still had great plans; in the power struggle of the Western Roman Empire you became first or you were nothing.

"Sire, how could the barbarians conquer the great city of Carthage, the most beautiful city in the west?"

Marcian nodded to the young man. "You're right, it is not only the most beautiful, but also the third largest city in the Empire, after Constantinople and Rome."

"We should drink the amphora wine before the sun rises, for then wine no longer tastes good." Vitus filled each of the men's goblets to the brim. "I don't want to appear immodest," Vitus said, slightly boastful, "but I was, after all, part of the king's success."

"I know," growled Marcian, suddenly cold. "But are you sure you didn't betray Rome with your actions?"

"Watch your tongue, Marcius. I didn't know what I was to be used for back then. Besides, Carthage was technically still in the hands of the Vandals, even for the last years I was with them on my own. Gaiseric finally released me, after almost thirty years of captivity."

"And friendship with him and time in his service," Macius snapped.

Vitus looked at the general cold as ice. "I beg your pardon, but there is still a Roman general and senator before you!"

Theodoric quickly kneeled before Vitus. "Please, Sire, let us not end the night in strife. Please tell me the story of how could Carthage be taken by these barbarians!" Vitus wiped the wine from his mouth, looked briefly into the piercing-cold eyes of Marcian, who had leaned far back on his canapé, and continued. "The city of Carthage was not conquered by Gaiseric, as he had actually been able to take it by trickery.

It was the night before the Festival of the Blessed Virgin Mary, which we Romans celebrate throughout the Empire. The taverns were already full days and nights before, the whole city in a festive frenzy. This was not unusual for a city like Carthage, which with all its sins was already the scapegoat of the empire. Gaiseric had secretly snuck many men into the city on these nights, all pretending to be traders loaded with sacks of gold coins. They spent a lot of money, especially on bribing and inviting soldiers, and the wine flowed like a stream. Furthermore there were ambassadors from Ravenna in the city who met officially with Huneric to negotiate a trade agreement about grain deliveries. The Vandals were ready to sell large quantities of grain cheaply to the Romans, as they were still dependent on the annona in Rome.

So the whole city was quite busy with itself, but Gaiseric had a plan, and I must confess that I played a not insignificant role in this matter. I and some other Romans in Gaiseric's service were brought in Roman clothes onto a Roman trireme, where we pretended to be Roman officials; then late at night we sailed on the ship directly into the port of Carthage. We convinced the port guards that we were coming directly from Rome with an important message from Aetius, addressed to the city governor of Carthage.

Of course, he was too drunk to speak at that point, intoxicated by Huneric's traders. We said we could not wait, as we had accommodations waiting in the city, and our ship had leaked. And so it happened; we were in town with only a few men. The farthest thing from our minds was sleep."

"Oh, Vitus, then you finally had a chance to speak to the governor so you could get into Roman service again?"

Vitus laid his hand on Theodoric's shoulder. "My boy, don't you think that after all these decades they had surely forgotten me? I had to do what I did; you should know that the city of Carthage at that time was full of thieves, whores, and people without God or morals. Here I wanted to help Gaiseric, because he would take action and free us Romans from sin and burden in that city."

Marcian jumped up as if stung by a scorpion. "Traitor! I knew it! You'll pay for this!"

"Calm down, great general. I am no traitor; let me explain. The men from the ship did not go to sleep in the inns, but crept to the Lion's Gate; the guards were first offered wine, and the unwilling ones were slaughtered without a sound.

So the gate was in the hands of the Vandals at sunrise, and the Vandal warriors, who had already taken up quarters not far from the city, marched that morning through the open gates in full formation, quiet and disciplined. The most important strategic points of the city and the port were already occupied. There was no battle at all, for the barbarians fooled the Romans, saying that they had been invited to save them from the Berbers, and soon the emperor himself would come and reward everyone. Of course, the Vandals were secretly laughing at their trickery. Since then, the great old lady of Africa, as we called the city, has belonged to the Vandals. Today I believe sooner or later the city would have been lost anyway, Marcian."

Marcian shook his head in disgust and disbelief. "For me you are as Roman as a barbarian. I don't want to know you anymore."

Vitus tried to calm him. "Don't say this; we go back a long way, Marcian! Let's empty the last amphora now, my old companion and my young future king!"

Marcian just shook his head and muttered under his breath. "Traitor."

Theodoric looked with unease at his teacher. "Sire, maybe you shouldn't talk so openly."

Vitus took a deep drink directly out of the amphora of wine. "You know who I am and why they call me Vitus Maximus! Once I had convinced the governor of our mission and helped Gaiseric, I was rewarded after years of deprivation and imprisonment. As a token of my freedom and as a friendly thanks to my services, he presented me with a Vandalic ceremonial shield with an embossed pattern of gilded bronze, which normally only high princes receive. I was given a few small bags with gold coins as well, of course. He also made sure I received a high ranking position here in Rome. Since then I have enjoyed my pension and senatorial life here in Rome and have been teaching royal students."

Theodoric and Marcian shook their heads, each for his own reason.

"Listen to me as I finish the story. The point was, the Vandals had conquered Carthage without bloodshed. And the takeover was well organized. The Vandals brought moral order to the city, and many taverns and brothels were burned to ashes. Anyone caught lying and cheating by the Vandals was punished in a barbaric manner."

Marican interrupted harshly. "Vitus, you know for a fact that almost the entire Roman fleet was lost to the barbarians when the city was taken by the Vandals. You contributed to that!"

"Gaiseric saved the city from decay," Vitus replied defiantly. "I can also tell you that Gaiseric also had great respect for the breathtaking Roman achievements, mainly for their old buildings and their imposing fortifications, which now in Vandal hand meant there was a new bulwark against the non-Christian Berbers. Gaiseric also wanted to create an opposite to Rome with its mixed population. He succeeded in doing this by expelling the dark-skinned Berbers and Nubians; I also believe that the people of Carthage are much happier among the Vandals than among the hated tax collectors from Rome."

# Chapter XVIII

The summer morning seemed strangely calm. There was neither the typical twittering of birds nor the humming of dragonflies to be heard, which normally buzzed around the garden pond of Vitus' villa in dozens. And although the sky was deep blue, there was a certain turbidity in the light; the inner courtyard of his villa also seemed unusually hot to him. Vitus was no longer really interested in his gardening hobby and was about to take his first rest. The peace was interrupted when suddenly a guard appeared in the courtyard.

"Vitus, your pupil is back."

Behind the guard, a tall young man in a toga appeared. Vitus smiled at the man like a lost son. "Theodoric, you're back!" Vitus said, delighted. The two men grasped each other at the forearms in greeting. "How many years has it been since we last met?

"Too long, Vitus; we must speak."

Vitus waved him down the marble hall. "I thank you for the visit, but let us speak in the coolness of the hall. Somehow the weather today is a bad omen. Wine, young man?"

"Not today, Sire. I must leave soon; as you know, my people need me."

"Of course. And besides, as you know, Rome is no longer safe."

Theodoric nodded. "Can Marcian help Rome?"

"Flavius Marcian has been Emperor in Constantinople for three years."

"Unbelievable. A fantastic career..."

"And he has kept his word to King Gaiseric to this day," interrupted Vitus.

"Not to wage war against the Vandals?"

"Exactly. As you know, Rome needs peace now more than anything, since Flavius Aetius, the greatest Magister Militum of all time, was murdered by the Emperor."

Suddenly footsteps echoed down the hall, and from the dark end of the marble hall soldiers ran toward them. A centurion of the palace guard approached frantically.

"General Marcian, we must get you and everyone here to safety. You must leave Rome at once!"

Marcian rose. "What happened?"

"Before Portus stands a fleet. You must leave right now. Direct order from the emperor himself!"

Vitus threw his wine cup in the corner. "What fleet? Have the Greeks now turned against Rome?"

"No Sire, the fleet of Vandals is at the gates of Rome, and there are no more troops to stop the barbarians. Gaiseric will occupy Rome!"

"Guards, come over, take the young man to safety!"

The young Theodoric was frightened as he was led out of the villa.

"If something happens to this young prince we do not need to fear the Vandals, as Constantinople will send executioners," Vitus yelled to the guards.

Marcian ran both hands through his hair. "You're right, Vitus. Now we must get out of here, preferably out of town."

"It's probably locked down already. I have a better idea. Besides, I'm sure nothing will happen to us, Marcian."

"You think we're safe because you know Gaiseric?"

"Perhaps, but there's also someone else the Vandals respect. Let us go now!"

The news of the landing of a huge Vandal fleet caused panic in the eternal city. The angry citizens gathered on the forum in front of the Imperial palace. The Emperor was called out loudly.

"Where are the legions that can protect us? What is the emperor doing now to avert the imminent danger?" they shouted.

Others gathered their belongings together to flee, but they did not know which direction to turn. The people ran screaming, confused and almost mad with fear. Too much had been heard of the atrocities of the barbarians.

When the commander of the Praetorian guard told
Emperor Maximus of the invasion, his eyes widened with
fear.

"What are you saying? The Vandals are attacking Rome?
How long will it be before they get here?"

"They say they're advancing at great speed. We
expect them outside our gates in the evening."

Emperor Maximus' lips trembled. "Is there anything we
can do?"

"No, my Caesar. Your predecessor Valentian sent all
available legionaires to Gaul and Illyricum against the Huns.
Even if all legions were to return immediately, it would take
them at least three weeks to reach Rome."

Emperor Maximus stared at the man in fear and disbelief.
"How many troops do we have here?"

"There'll be about two hundred men, perhaps even less.
They are scattered throughout the city to protect public
buildings. Most of them are stationed here, to protect the
palace. They're securing the entrances right now because the

people are angry and frightened. They demand that the emperor protect them."

Maximus laughed desperately. "Demand that I protect them? But who will protect me? I must escape, now. Get everything ready. I will leave the palace through the back entrance. I need a carriage for the Imperial treasure."

The commander bowed. "Shall the empress and her daughters go with you, your Majesty?"

"There's no time for that. They will not harm her, but they will nail me to the gate and let the crows eat me up. Now get my carriage!"

The officer hurried away and Maximus ran to his chambers. He gathered his jewelry and gold coins together, put them in leather bags and tied as many to his body as he could. He was preparing to leave when Empress Eudocia entered.

"What's going on in Rome? People are upset. Are you leaving?"

Maximus laughed mockingly. "Yes, I am going on a journey - the Vandals are forcing me to. They're almost at the gates of Rome."

Eudocia's eyes widened. "The Vandals? But how is that possible? Will you flee like a coward and do nothing about them? What about me and my daughters?"

"I can't take you with me. That would slow me down too much. Now get out of my way! I've lost enough time already."

Eudocia's bewilderment now turned into cold rage. "I have always known that you are only a coward. Go without me, as I prefer a life as a prisoner of the barbarians to a life by your side!"

Before he could answer, she had run out of the room.

"Women!" he growled. Then he hurried down the steps to the exit at the back of the palace. The commander had already gotten the carriage, but he hadn't considered that an Imperial carriage would cause suspicion among the angry citizens. So it came about that an angry mob had followed the carriage in rage. They were ready to let their wrath out on the emperor.

"There he is, that traitor, leaving us to our fate!" A voice shouted, and someone threw a stone.

The emperor tried to hide himself inside the carriage as best as he could. He stuck his head out to shout at his guards. "Praetorians, form a protective ring around the carriage," he ordered.

One of the Praetorians, whose tall stature and Nordic face clearly showed his origins, stepped forward looked at the emperor in contempt.

"I am Ursus, head of the Praetorian Guard. I tell you all, we will not protect a cowardly Caesar who will flee in secret. Rome deserves better than that!"

Maximus interrupted Ursus in his speech. "Kill this insurgent and get the people out of the way!"

Ursus yelled back. "Death to the cowardly tyrant who betrayed Rome!"

He knelt to the ground and reached for a small cobblestone. "You don't even deserve to die by the sword!"

With these words he threw the stone at Maximus with tremendous force, so quickly that the emperor could not avoid it. The stone hit Maximus on the temple and he stumbled out of the carriage and fell onto the pavement. The crowd roared and their last inhibitions fell. Angry hands reached for Maximus, dragged him and beat him with fists and stones. So it happened that the Patrician Petronius Maximus, who had weaseled his way up to Caesar by murder, was stoned to death by the mob as the Praetorians watched. But death wasn't enough for the crowd. They dragged his body through the streets down to the Tiber and threw what was left of his mortal remains into the river.

Gaudentius, the son of the murdered Magister Militum general Aetius, had noticed the unrest outside from his window of the senatorial lodge. Suddenly the Empress Eudocia rushed in.

"The Vandals are about to attack Rome and Maximus is fleeing! If you want to get to safety, I can make sure you get into the Imperial carriage!"

Gaudentius remained calm. "My Empress, your husband Caesar Maximus has just been beaten to death by the angry citizens of Rome as he tried to flee in his carriage, just as you suggested. I saw it with my own eyes. Our Praetorian Guard did not protect him either."

Eudocia froze and started to sob. "He deserved it; I'm not crying for him. Gaudentius, you are the future of Rome if there still is any. Get away from here; the palace will be the first to be stormed by the barbarians. I must stay because I represent the Empire now. But please take my daughters Placidia and Eudoxia with you, for I do not want them to fall into the hands of these monsters."

"I will see to it that they are brought to safety. I will reassure you as well. My father and I know that King Gaiseric is not a cruel man. I have sent a messenger to Pope Leo. I'm sure he and an influential senator will help us."

# Chapter XIX

In the basilica dedicated to the last disciple of Jesus, Saint Peter, Pope Leo knelt before the altar and prayed. "Lord, your trials are hard. You sent this Antichrist to test our faith. I bow my head in humility; my faith remains firm in your goodness and mercy. I pray not for myself, but for this holy city consecrated to you. Do not let them perish in destruction and fire and spare the bodies and lives of the people here. You are the true God who made heaven and earth. We place our lives in your hands."

Leo rose, bowed his head before the cross at the altar and crossed himself. When he turned around, he looked into the eyes of the high council of bishops standing in the back row. They all were agitated and afraid.

"I know about your worries." Pope Leo tried to reassure them as he approached them, but their spokesman stepped forward to contradict him.

"You certainly do not know this yet, Your Holiness, the people of Rome are overwhelmed with fear and anger, they

have stoned the emperor and thrown him into the Tiber
because he wanted to flee with the Imperial treasure and leave
the citizens to their fate."

"The emperor is dead?"

"Yes. Now, Your Holiness, you are the only authority in
this city. You have to talk to the the people and calm them
down, or anarchy will come."

Pope Leo folded his hands and looked upwards. "The Lord
has given me a sign!  I will do anything in my power to save
this city from greater harm, so help me God."

"The bishops are at your disposal, Your Holiness."

"Follow me and let people know that I want to talk to
them. Get the message out to gather in the square in front of
St. Peter's Cathedral."

It didn't take much to get the citizens of Rome to St. Peter's
Square. The news that the Holy Father himself wanted to
speak to them gave them hope. Soon the square was filled,
and the frightened people looked up expectantly to the
balustrade from which the Holy Father always showed
himself to the people and gave his blessing.

Pope Leo shouted as loud as he could so that as many people as possible could hear him. He was sure that all who heard would pass on his words.

"The Lord is the light, the truth and the life," he began. "Go home and wait for the things to come. Pray to the Lord that misfortune may pass you by. I myself will confront the barbarians to pray for the preservation of the city. If this is not in His counsel, then accept His punishment without complaint, for God forgives your sins and welcomes you into His kingdom. Go in peace!" The message spread slowly, but eventually the people of the city calmed down. The Holy Father would stand up for them. That was the only hope they now clung to. Slowly the crowd dispersed and followed the Pope's words.

King Gaiseric had his army march in rows of six, using the entire width of the Via Portuensis. They had taken their time; six hundred ships laid secured in Portus and waited to be loaded with plunder and slaves, while some of the ships rowed alongside the army on the Tiber. Not a single Roman soldier intercepted their march. It was already late afternoon as they reached the Aurelian Walls. With the sound of horns the army stopped briefly at the mighty double arches of the Porta Portuensis.

Gaiseric was surprised at the complete silence at the open gate, and he felt an unusual calm for such a significant day. In the distance, a group appeared at the Porta. They weren't close enough yet to see what was going on, but one could see the flashing of Roman parade uniforms as they were worn in victory parades from times long gone by. Gaiseric closed his eyes and shook his head. Did they prepare for resistance?

His youngest son Gento galloped towards him and stopped at his side. "They go into battle with a parade carriage," he mocked, for his sharp eyes had spotted a ceremonial carriage behind the feathered riders. Gaiseric rode to the front, and as he did so he noticed a white flag in the hand of the foremost horseman.

"They want to negotiate," Gaiseric said, not particularly surprised. "We will ride towards them. The rest wait here!"

Huneric protested immediately. "I will accompany you with guards. If any of them make even one false move, it will be his last."

Gaiseric smiled. "Of course you will be near me and fulfill your task. I have become so accustomed to your presence that I no longer need to ask."

Huneric nodded contentedly and waved at the men selected for this assignment.

The carriage had stopped. The riders made way as an elderly man in a white robe with a large golden cross around his neck emerged from the carriage. On his head he wore a flat, round cap.

The man raised both hands and bowed as a sign of submission.

Gaiseric rode a little closer. He kept an eye on the magnificently dressed Roman officers, but they kept their distance from the man in white and did not move.

"Who are you to dare stand in my way? I am Gaiseric, king of the Vandals and Alans. Rome will fall into my hands today and there is nothing you can do to stop me. So, what do you want from me?"

"I am Leo, the representative of God on earth and the successor of Saint Peter as the chief shepherd of the believers of this world."

Gaiseric waved the Arian high priest Tirias to himself and asked whether the little man before them was really the Pope. Tirias confirmed quietly. Gaiseric turned again to the Pope. "As you surely know, I am not one of your believers. I adhere to the Arian faith, the supreme shepherd of which is here by my side. So why did you come?"

Pope Leo snuck a quick look at Tirias. Of course he knew him from the reports of the bishops of Hippo Regius and Carthage. "I don't want to argue about our different beliefs now, as that would be presumptuous of me in my situation. I stand here before you to pray for this city."

Gaiseric's face tightened. "Where is the emperor? Is he hiding under the skirts of the church now? Only he alone can hand this city over to me."

"That's no longer possible. He was stoned to death by the angry crowds when he tried to escape. I am the only authority here in Rome."

"Maximus is dead?" Gaiseric looked at Huneric, who was visibly irritated.

Pope Leo raised his hands higher. "Look at this holy city. God, the Lord, has made this city the cradle of true faith. In this city Peter, the disciple of the Lord Jesus Christ, walked and gave strength and confidence to the martyrs. God will not want you to destroy the testimonies of his work."

Gaiseric moved his horse up beside the Pope, shaking his head in disapproval. "Don't you know a better reason than this? It is precisely the martyrs who remind me how mercilessly the Romans have treated all those who did not bow to their will. So why should I spare them?"

At that moment, general Gaudentius and Gaiseric's old friend Vitus stepped out of the carriage. They both bowed deeply before Gaiseric, who flinched in surprise but then nodded to them with a smile.

"So here we meet again. What are you doing here, Vitus?"

"Forgive our unexpected appearance, Sire. We wanted to accompany the Pope because we have something to tell you."

"Then be brief, Vitus, for as you can see I am busy," Gaiseric said with a smug smile.

"My king, I believe it is beneath you to destroy this beautiful city."

"Who says I want to destroy this city? When have I ever destroyed a city, Vitus?"

"Sire, you are now the ruler of Rome. Through the millennium-old history of the city, each ruler has given something for Rome and each has made it a little better and more beautiful. I ask you to spare the inhabitants and beautiful buildings, that's all."

Gaiseric shifted restlessly on his saddle and stared at Vitus. "You are quite a strange bunch; have I not helped you to high offices and wealth, yet you are allied against me with these Catholics?" After a few seconds of silence Geiseric moved closer to Vitus, and asked in a more sinister tone, "Are you with them, or with us?"

Vitus just shook his head silently and for a moment Vitus and Geiseric's eyes locked. Geiseric leaned close and whispered, "I cannot even speak of how disappointed I am in you."

"High Lord and King," Marcian interrupted. "Will you promise that the population will be spared and the city will be preserved? The emperor in Constantinople will appreciate it."

Gaiseric's gaze darkened. "Listen. I will take what I need and want. I will take anything of worth in this city including as many slaves as possible, and if something doesn't suit me, be it a person or a building, it won't exist anymore. Do I have to make myself any more clear?"

The Pope knelt and folded his hands. "But then what shall we have left?"

"Your lives," hissed Gaiseric, and signaled his army to move forward.

***